I0519489

FINDING MY HAPPINESS

What would you do with a fresh start?

Kiki Holstad

Kiki Holstad

This book is dedicated to anyone looking for a sign to keep going.
I also want to thank Fluffypandas, Babybiscuit, and AlexisR for always believing in me. I love you guys.

CONTENTS

IMPORTANT

~*~Dear Readers~*~

These stories play like movies in my head, so that is
how I write them. I do not utilize AI so I apologize in
advance for any errors, wordiness, or boredom that
you may experience when reading this book.

In this fictional reality, history is a bit different. 150 years ago,
the world united for peace. Due to this, medical advancements
have eradicated: heart disease, various viruses, cancers,
stds, sickle cell, and many other chronic illnesses.

This led to a drastic birth decline, but it also
extended the average lifespan.
The average cost of living is lower, and the quality
of goods has improved drastically.
Any similarities between the book's reality and
your own, are purely coincidental.
Warning:
Some blood mentioned in later chapters
~*~Dear Readers~*~

Blurb

Two weeks after turning thirty, Sabrina Eldwin was offered a settlement from the company she gave ten years of her life to. After settling her debts, she hands her keys over to her landlord and sets off on a journey of self-discovery. A month of chef prepared meals at a cabin in the mountains is just what she needs to figure out what to do next. Picnics under the stars, guided hikes, shopping, hot tubs, and endless appetizers await, or so she thought. Running into a not-so-burned-out old flame while fantasizing about the retreat owner was not what she expected to do. Determined to make the best of her first vacation in ten years, she vows to control her wandering hands. Feeling up a bronze statue should be okay though, right? How will she survive her journey of self-discovery with so many distractions?
*Warning Mildly Spicy
*Slice of Life/Wholesome

CHAPTER ONE

~Sabrina~

Monday October 13th
9:30am

As I walk up to the podium, I think back on what brought me here. *I was asked to give a presentation on why career longevity at Exco would be a great personal investment.* They chose me because I had recently celebrated my 10-year anniversary of joining Exco. The 'party' the company threw me ended early with me fighting off my drunk boss in the conference room. *They didn't know about that last part though, yet.* I look up at Beth in the tech booth; she gives me an encouraging smile. *I'm glad she has my back and will keep the microphone on.* Mira at HR assured me she wouldn't face too much backlash over this. *As long our plan worked, that is.* I lean towards the microphone "I quit". My face flushes from excitement as the words fall from my mouth in a rush. I look over and see Mr. Quick standing in the corner, his mouth hanging open in shock. A thin sheen of sweat already covers his pale face.

I hold up my resignation notice I sent to HR 30 days prior and add, "However, I would still like to honor my prior commitment: To give a presentation on the benefits of working at Exco long-term." I hear someone yell to 'cut the mic' and I begin. Mr. Quick starts to turn red as security surrounds the stage. *I have maybe 2 minutes before they realize security is on our side.* "I first started working for Exco 10 years ago. I was a part-timer in the mail room with the goal of working my way towards retiring at Exco as an executive manager." A man in a suit walks over to Mr. Quick, and they conversate in hushed voices.

2

"After I finished my degree, I was promoted to full-time in the mailroom." A few people clap sarcastically and I smile. "I had high hopes of transferring departments once I had my degree in hand. After a few months, my hard work paid off and I was moved up to the temp department."

I look around at the people now recording my speech, "I expected some distance between co-workers. Maybe working overtime here and there on projects and giving up weekends to build rapport etc. I wasn't expecting the number of coffees I had to purchase for my bosses that I was never reimbursed for. I also wasn't prepared for the hazing between coworkers, or the deliberate withholding of information in order to sabotage coworkers. The worst part was that the internal battles were spurred on by higher ups for amusement." A few people stand and turn to leave as I continue. "Being told that I needed to volunteer most of my weekends, sometimes without notice and sometimes unpaid, was also unexpected." I glance at Beth and see a dark figure talking to her through the tech booth door. *Please be ok.* I leaned towards the microphone to continue.

"Eventually I worked my way through various departments as a temp agent doing everything from secretarial work to running errands for clients. Mr. Brooks noticed my hardwork and offered me a full-time position in his office as a secretary. For the past five years; he has forced me to work after hours on various projects *without pay*, laid hands on me when sober *and* drunk at multiple events, called me at all hours for non-work *and* work purposes, threatened to fire me, and left a voicemail threatening to have me blacklisted if I spoke against him. I have everything documented right here." I hold up the flash drive and look at the shocked faces around me. More security guards form a tighter circle around the stage "I took the liberty of already submitting it to HR a few minutes before walking up here". I look up and see a grinning Beth, giving me a thumbs up as a security guard is talking to her through the door. "This moment is for those who are afraid to speak up." I turn to Mr. Quick and lean towards the microphone "Please stop your harassment and let me live my life." I step away from the podium as people start to talk amongst themselves.

The security team escorts Mr. Quick away as Simi Pompusa pulls me into a hug before saying, "You did great. My turn." She confidently walks over to the microphone and introduces herself before telling her story. The tall man that was talking to Mr. Quick earlier, smiles at me before walking over. "We'll make sure there are no interruptions, so long as everyone remains mindful that families may watch this. Remain polite." He taps his nose and his dark eyes sparkle with mischief. A line of people starts forming behind the podium. Each person different from the next in almost every way, yet all had a similar story; Exco protected the people that abused them. We all met via an online support group back in April. Upon finding out we had similar experiences; we agreed to gather evidence and meet at Exco's 'New Frontier' conference to expose how rotten the company really is. I flash Layla a supportive smile and she quickly looks away. Her hands fidget by her sides as her brown eyes look around the room. I think about how far we have come and how much we relied on her.

For 6 months we budgeted every penny we had to ensure our separate debts were paid in full before embarking on this next chapter of our lives. It's something Layla stood firm on and taught us how to budget accordingly. *I finished paying my student loans, car, credit cards, even my cellphone is fully paid for now. Granted, I only have $6,000 left in my savings account vs the $106,000 I had six months ago. I'm glad we estimated what each of us would need to carry us through whatever happens next.* We often joked about buying a large house somewhere and splitting the bills 'Golden Girls' style while we rebuild our lives. *I really hope this works, otherwise we may only have each other when this is all over.* My phone lights up with 'Alex' in bold letters on the front. I hit answer, bracing myself for the scolding I'm about to receive, "Hey Daddy".

Three days later

I blink multiple times to clear my eyes, yet my vision remains hazy. For the past few days, Alex has been going through all of my documentation to prepare for this meeting. *I didn't sleep well thanks to random bouts of maniacal laughter all night. Waking up at 2am to Daddy yelling 'I'll get you all' was unsettling to say the least. No more wine coolers for you.* Mr. Burgess clears his throat. "Do you have any questions about the first page?" He asks patiently. I nod, "Can you go over it again but with a little more detail, please?" I ask and Daddy frowns as though to say 'Why are you entertaining this? We want to take them to court'. I shake my head, wanting the time to collect myself.

"Certainly Miss Eldwin. I trust you understand that if you accept this settlement, you agree to cut all ties with Exco and will henceforth be held liable should you discuss anything related to Exco, or your time at the company, with anyone outside of this room." I nod and he continues, "Mr. Quick has already been banned from all properties and blacklisted from any future employment opportunities with Exco and it's affiliates. I am unable to disclose additional details about his case at this time. As a show of good faith, Exco agrees to provide you with a glowing recommendation, to use at your discretion of course." I sigh in relief. *Thanks to the internet, everyone seems to know what happened at the seminar.*

I look at Alex, her dark eyes shining as she looks at Mr. Burgess with a determined expression. I can tell she is going to tear their offer apart and demand fair retribution, or we go to court. At 34, Alexandra Hillman was already competing for partner at a local firm, and she was gaining ground *quickly*. She earned the nickname of "Daddy" after her debut in court. She slides a water bottle over to me. Sensing my discomfort, she glances at me. 'Be patient, I have a plan' she screams with her eyes. *Fine by me, I know nothing about any of this. My duties were answering the phone, scheduling, editing, and secretarial work. Oh, and getting coffee. I was really good at that.*

Mr. Burgess clears his throat after noticing that I wasn't focused anymore. I straighten as he says, "Additionally, Exco will honor partial retirement pay in the sum of $3,000. This is after taxes are withheld and will be paid to you on the first of each month. Exco will continue to provide medical coverage as part of their retirement package. You will not lose these benefits unless you break this agreement. Exco will pay $25,000 for relocation expenses as well as a final settlement of $250,000 for any hardships incurred at your time at Exco due to unpaid overtime, faulty leadership/management..." He continues, but his words start blending together.

I shake my head and immediately jot my name down. Alex coughs, but I ignore her. *I mean really, what is there to discuss? I get paid to move anywhere I want, have retirement pay and benefits secured 2 weeks after turning thirty, and I get $250,000 to start over somewhere else!* I flip through the pages, and sign on the lines as Alex coughs again, louder this time. Being raised in a low-income household had me foaming at the mouth over their offer. "Sabrina, may I have a word with you?" Daddy asks while tapping her dark, slender fingers on the table. *I can feel the daggers being thrown from those gorgeous eyes of hers, but I won't do it. I won't look at her. No one can resist Daddy when she's doing business.* "No thank you Alex, I believe I've got it. Mr. Burgess what is the next step?" I say as casually as possible, as though I wasn't squealing inside while picturing lavish spreads next to a shaded hot tub in the mountains. *All knowledge and experience gained in my 30 years of life have flown the coop.*

CHAPTER TWO

~Sabrina~
One month later

"Can you please stop sighing and help me pack instead?" I ask while glancing at my stuff strewn all over the floor. Alex slides me a dirty look, "Excuse me for still being upset. With the piles of records you kept, I could have negotiated enough money for you to buy the building. You wouldn't have needed to pack or clean anything. Could have just rented the place out or used it for storage." She pauses then turns towards me, "You could have easily hired a moving company, even with the settlement you got. Why didn't you?" She crosses her arms and waits for my reply. "I wanted to say goodbye to my life here, and spend more time with you of course" her lips twitch before she turns to the kitchen. "I won't help pack, but I will help myself to more of those canned bubblies". I laugh as she opens my fridge in search of a mango flavored beverage. "I was tired, overworked, underpaid, and desperate for change. I didn't want a long battle, I just wanted to start my new life. Can you really blame me?" She huffs and I pout in response, "They dangled my weakness in front of me, financial security. You know how I was raised, three grand a month could support me while I figure out my life. I could get a van and travel while writing books. Maybe I'll paint by the beach or a lake somewhere. The world is my oyster now" I smile and toss my toiletries bag into my suitcase. I do a victory pose as it lands perfectly between my neck-pillow and silk pillowcases.

Alex walks over and places her hand on my forehead, as though she was in search of a fever "Who are you and where is my Brini?" She asks with concern filling her voice. "You don't

7

like to write and you can barely draw a stick person. I can't think of a single hobby that you have, other than eating snacks and running." I pout as she continues, "Forget cooking. You also said you never want to live in a hurricane zone again." She huffs as I gently take her hand off my forehead and reply. "True but I've always wanted to have a movie-like vacation to the mountains. I could hike or learn to snowboard. I can at least check those off my list while I'm on vacation." I let go of her hand and turn to start packing before adding, "Now I have time to figure out what hobbies I like. I could be a prodigy in something, I'll never know unless I discover it. Also, I run to eat snacks, there is no love for running here" I place my new oversized hoodie next to my underwear sets. "I have no debt thanks to Layla's planning. I've sold or given away almost everything I own, that allows me a complete fresh start." Alex nods as she drinks her beverage. "I also need to figure out what I want to do. My month-long vacation should give me plenty of time to do that. No cooking, cleaning, or tv to interrupt me. I even splurged on scenic picnics. I reserved every class and amenity they offered, I won't leave without learning something at least." I say with a confident grin.

"You stress me so much, why do I put up with you?" Alex sighs dramatically while rolling her eyes. "Because you love me" I whine back at her and then toss her my red suit jacket. "Here, enjoy my favorite jacket. I hope you give it good memories" I say while wiping a fake tear. Alex laughs and walks past me. She grabs a bag from my closet and my mouth drops. "Where did you hide that?" I slowly walk towards her while looking her over. "I was here the entire time, and you didn't bring that in with you. At least not in your hands. Got anything else in there?" I start patting her sides gently as she laughs. "I wanted to get you something for your trip. I hope you enjoy these sweats with extra deep pockets." She hands me the black bag, and I scurry away squealing. *Perfect timing since I donated all of my old clothes!*

"Thank you, Daddy!" *I love deep pockets!* I reach into the bag and pull out the gray hoodie. "It's so soft. Oh look, it has light pink flowers that match the stitching" I look over while

8

pointing at the flowers. She put it on so fast. I laugh as she leans towards the mirror, "Mmm I have wanted this baby for years. Don't worry, Daddy will treat you so much better" she says as she looks into the mirror. The deep red of the jacket matched her lipstick and the bottom of her pumps perfectly. She looks at me and purses her lips, "Girl this was made for me. I should have snatched this from you ages ago" I nod in agreement. *She was right, her brown skin looked gorgeous against the deep red of the jacket. If I were into women, forget the jacket, she would have snatched my soul ages ago.* I shake my head and smile.

"You really should pack more though, what if something happens along the way to your cabin? Do you have any means of protection against bears? The backpack I mailed last week should be in the post office by now. It's by the airport." She adds as she pulls out her phone to verify the delivery time. "It arrived yesterday. What time do you land? You are renting a Jeep, right?" She continues before I can answer, "I should take off work and come with you. I can get a ticket right now." She says as she types on her phone. *Oh no, she'll get fired.* I walk over to her, "Alex, you can't leave when you're in the middle of a big case. Especially when you are working with the head of the firm" I push her phone down slowly and add, "I'll be fine, I promise I packed the essentials. I'll order more stuff to be delivered to my cabin while waiting to board my flight. I have a long layover, so I plan to get extra sleep during that as well as on the flight. I will be refreshed for the drive so there is no need to worry." Alex nods and throws her can in the recycling bin. "I should land and get my rental, which yes is a Jeep, around 8am. It should take me a few hours to get to Boulder Springs, depending on how many stops I make. Check in is at 8pm, which would be 10pm here. That gives me plenty of time to shop and get all sorts of goodies" I pause as I find myself drooling at the thought of getting to buy an entire wardrobe while on vacation.

Wiping my mouth with my sleeve, I hand Alex the last sparkling mango juice. She thanks me and says "Tell me again about the place you are going to. I want to know exactly what you plan to do in the middle of nowhere for a month". She pauses to drink her beverage as I scan through the cupboards. Before I can reply she adds, "Everything should wrap up with this case soon. Then I can join you for the holiday banquet in a few weeks. Expect me to show up if 5 days go by with no word from you though". I open my closet again, still expecting to see it full. "You know, I don't think I'd be surprised if you did that." I close the door and do a final look over my bedroom. "Just show up I mean. If you do, please bring your own coffee. You always complain about mine" I say with a laugh as I close the bedroom door. I walk over to the couch as she stands. "Also, it isn't in the middle of nowhere, there are other cabins around and a few cafes. I think..." I bite my lip as I try to remember what was nearby.

She walks over to my whiteboard and grabs the pink marker. "Things to get before my last first vacation: 2 weeks of clothes, 1 week of groceries, first aid kit, emergency supplies, snow survival gear." I sigh as dramatically as I can and pluck the marker gently from her fingertips. "Come on, it isn't that bad. I will send pictures of everything. If you can't get them due to bad service, then I will write you an extremely detailed letter every day." I wipe off the board and add, "It isn't supposed to snow for a few more days, so I have plenty of time to get settled in and buy tons of ffafs." As I say the f's quickly, I grin. Alex turns towards me "Ffafs means what exactly?" I laugh as she imitates me. "Food, firewood, and fun stuff' I say as I dodge the pillow she flings at me.

"Why am I even here?" she says as she grabs her purse. "We have been over this Alex." I exhale slowly and take her hand. She turns and looks at me as I reply, "You are my platonic soulmate." She laughs and takes her hand back. "True, but seriously what else do you need? The apartment is completely empty except for this one suitcase. "We are all done boo. We even drank the last can of bubbles" I look around, and she is right. *I really am done. It's time to start my first real vacation, with no chance of work interrupting. I'm officially a freelancer.* My stomach twists as the excitement and nervousness fight for dominance in my belly. *I'm 30 years old, and I still don't feel like a proper 'adult'. I have a guaranteed income of $3,000 per month with no debt and tons of opportunities in front of me. So what exactly do I do and how do I even start?* I smack my head on the wall, less gently than I intend which snaps Alex to attention. "Girl what are you doing? Stop that" she leads me back to the couch and sits down with me. "Everything will be okay. You've been a workaholic for so long, you never even learned to cook." She pats my leg in sympathy before adding "Which makes sense, you were in college since you were basically 14 years old" I start to correct her over exaggeration, "I definitely wasn't 14-". She snaps her fingers, "Don't interrupt me. That's just rude, you know better". She scolds me and I immediately apologize, "Yes Daddy." She laughs and I grin back at her.

Her eyes start to glisten and I frown. "Al what's really going on?" She crosses her arms as she stands and begins to pace behind the couch. "I won't see you for an entire month. What if you decide to move across the country? What am I supposed to do, just follow you there?" Alex slows her pacing, then stops. "Okay new plan; You do your thing this month and let me know where you decide on. I'll do research and see what it would take to open a firm in that area". She grabs my arm and pulls me up before I can fully register her words. "Maybe this is my nudge to stop chasing other people's dreams and start following my own. I had a goal of making partner here at DHC&T for so long, I never stopped to think about other options. I don't even like their work ethics! I love you Brini, and I will see you at the banquet. Who knows, maybe even sooner" She winks at me then turns to grab her purse. "Wait, Alex-" before I can finish, she is out the door and down the hall.

My word she can really move in those heels. She wasn't serious, there's no way. She has been with DHC&T since she graduated from Tulane. I wheel my suitcase behind me, pausing to scan the small one-bedroom apartment I called home for the last 3 years. *The only other places I lived, I had shared with other people. This was the first place I lived on my own.* Glimpses of holidays and various memories spent here flash before my eyes. I smile and close the door behind me before heading down the hall. *I don't want to miss my future by mulling over my past. Look at me adulting like a pro, I've got this. Alex is freaking out over nothing.* I smile and press the elevator down button.

CHAPTER THREE

~Sabrina~

November 13th
10:30am

I do not have this. **Why are there no guard rails on the mountain roads?** I breathe slowly, trying to stop mental spiral. *Why would anyone think this was safe? What about us non-mountain folk who have only witnessed the flat lands, huh? How do I even get down the-* I shake my head and loosen my grip on the steering wheel. *Spiraling will not help my current situation. I simply have to look straight ahead and not look down at all. Not even a smidgen of a bit.* I exhale slowly. *I can do this. I deserve some time to rest my body, mind, and spirit. I have been through a lot and I welcome the chance to heal as well as grow.* "Started in the mail room and now we're here" I chuckle. *Breathe in, breathe out.* "I am filled with opportunity and-" I brace myself for a quick death as a giant truck passes me quickly, shaking the entire vehicle. I blink rapidly as images of the Jeep rolling down the mountain flood my mind. "You know what? I think a valley vacation would be excellent this time of year. The weather looked gorgeous down there and I saw so many cute towns." I instantly perk up while I look for a safe spot to turn around. *Time to go back down the mountain and shop my worries away.*

I jump as "GPS signal lost" comes through my speakers. "That's fine, I can just turn around and go back the way I came" I reply cheerfully. I glance out of the window. *The scenery is amazing. If I must die here, at least I get to see a pretty view first.* I exhale slowly and remind myself this is a temporary setback. *Once I get to the valley, I'll call the retreat and let them know I've had a change of plans. If they don't want to refund me, then that's on me for canceling on the day of check in. What about everything I ordered though?* I sigh and then smile at the sun peeking through the trees. "That's a future me problem. Let's focus on turning around and getting a new place in the valley for tonight" I hum cheerily and pull into a scenic observation area. I climb out of the Jeep to look at the beautiful snow-capped mountains. *This is absolutely gorgeous.* The sky casts a purple hue onto the mountains, and I smile. *This is why I wanted to come here. Maybe one day I'll come back, in the summer though.*

3 hours later

It's snowing so much, I don't even know what road I'm on. "You are two miles from your destination." My GPS announces, startling me unnecessarily. I compose myself before replying, "Excuse me? What do you mean I am two miles from my destination?" I slow down as the windshield wipers start moving faster. "You couldn't find my destination for the past two and a half hours. How did I end up close to my destination? I can't-" I'm unable to finish my rant as my GPS suddenly interrupts with "TURN LEFT NOW!" I immediately jerk the wheel to the left, as though any other option would result in my untimely death. The Jeep slides and halts with a '***Thunk***'. I check to make sure I'm ok. *Thankfully the airbags didn't release, but what did I hit? A giant pile of snow? Maybe the mountain?* I look out the window hoping to see a sign or landmark, but everything is covered in white. *It would be incredibly beautiful if it wasn't going to become my gravesite.*

I pause to collect myself and exhale slowly, "Snow won't start for another few days? Lies." *Alex's pamphlet said to stay in the vehicle in case of a blizzard.* "Time to call for help." I look at my phone and groan. *Of course there's no service. Maybe the signal is blocked because of the snow?* I sigh in frustration. *Then how did the GPS work?* I type out 'Does snow block cell reception?' and wait. "The page can't be found?" *I see. Because I have no service.* I lean against the seat and close my eyes. *Common sense has left me, I'm doomed. How dare I ruin this gorgeous scenery with my corpse.* My eyes snap open as I remember the backpack in the back seat. *I can't believe Alex's doom-prepping may actually save me.* I grimace at the thought of her gloating. *As soon as she hears about this, I won't ever hear the end of it. She can never know.*

I start to look through the backpack, silently thanking her again "Wind up flashlight, wind up radio, solar charger, various adapters, jumper cables, spare batteries, MRE- *"Wait, how and when did Alex get an MRE?* I turn it over to read the bag. "Chili Mac?" I frown at the thought of having to go to the bathroom out here. *I'll pass for now.* I continue to search and pull out a foldable shovel. "This is so cute, it's like a baby shovel!" I squeal in delight. *Where did she find this?* I grin as I put my coat on, my spirit rejuvenated by the power of cuteness. *I'm glad I picked up this coat at the airport.* "Let's see if I can dig out the Jeep and get it to start. I've seen plenty of shows where a man shows up to save the day. Not today! I will be my own knight!" *Or knightess, whatever it's called.* I open the door and hop out into the fluffy snow, shocked at how high it's piled in such a short time..

Thirty minutes later

*Is this how I die? I can't die now; I **just** paid off my student loans.* I slam the hood closed in frustration. *I can't figure out why it won't start. Guess I do need saving after all.* I set out the flares in hopes of someone swooping in to save the day. After making sure there was no more snow on the Jeep, I climb back in. I shrug off my coat to make a pillow out of it. Next, I grab the heated blanket from the backpack and drape it over me. *The two hour battery time should last longer if I set it to auto off/on every 30 min.* I lean over and turn on the radio to finish my little nest as I wait for someone to drive by. "It's 2pm now so I should have about 4-5 hours until it gets dark. Hopefully someone will see the flares since it stopped snowing a few minutes ago." *Vacations with snow, permanently canceled. Going to the beach instead.* I start to think about relaxing on a covered balcony with a good book, as I am lulled to sleep by the radio.

Later

I jerk awake in the dark, terrified. *Did the power go out?* I shiver against the cold air. *Why is it so cold? I need a new mattress.* Groaning, I move to turn my bedside lamp on. Memories from earlier flood my mind as I realize I am still in the Jeep. *It wasn't a nightmare! Is it dark already? How long has it been?* I move my arms around as I sit up. I push against the door, but it's frozen shut. *I can't be buried under this much snow, no one will see the flares or the Jeep!* I focus my breathing to calm down and start to search blindly for a light source. Feeling my phone, I quickly turn it on. "Geez it's 6pm and still no signal. It shouldn't be this dark yet, so that means I really am buried in the snow." I grab the flashlight and start to wind it, reminding myself *again* to apologize to Alex and thank her for 'going overboard'. *If I survive that is.* After emptying out the rest of the backpack, I set up the hot pouches and MRE. *I'm so hungry, but what if I have to use the bathroom?* I look at the door again. "If I can get the door open, then maybe I can go find help or a cabin. I saw hundreds of cabins all over the place around here when looking up places to stay. Someone has to be close by." I start to put a plan together while my food heats.

Remembering what Alex said about bears, I start to question if I should open it when it's done cooking. *What if a bear smells this and comes looking for me? Will a questionable MRE satisfy it? Would I have to finish cooking it first?* "Sabrina you are not opening a food truck for a bear, get it together woman!" I clamp my hand over my mouth as I hear something moving outside. I turn off my flashlight and hug it to my chest. Suddenly a massive brown paw hits the window. Screaming, I scramble for the bag of food as a second paw hits the car "LET ME FINISH COOKING IT!" I yell, hoping it understands me. *I am **not** about to have an angry bear eat me because I didn't properly prepare their dinner.*

The paw continues swiping at the windows and door, snow blowing all around the massive creature. "WILL YOU KNOCK IT OFF WHILE I GET YOUR DINNER READY!" It goes quiet for a moment, and I check to make sure I haven't soiled myself. I really am about to open a food truck for a bear. I start thinking of a plan as the MRE continues to cook. After a while, the bear-thing starts hitting the door again. I scramble to open the bag. It continues hitting the door, shaking it slightly. The bear lets out a muffled roar as I hear a loud "POP". *Oh no, it broke the door!* I squeeze my eyes shut and yell "HERE! JUST TAKE IT!" Bracing myself for claws, I hold up the partially cooked MRE. *I should have listened to Daddy.*

CHAPTER FOUR

~Logan~

November 13th
5pm

'Snow expected to start falling late tonight' my foot. My phone rings, startling me. "Logan Hale speaking." I answer while loading the last bag into the bed of my truck. "Mr. Hale, are you aware of the road conditions?" Mr. Jenkins answers gruffly. Gregory Jenkins was a baker well into his 80s that refused to fully retire. *He loves nothing more than to gossip and complain about his neighbors.* I stop and look around at the snow falling heavily around me. I grimace as fluffy mounds form on top of the supplies I just loaded up. "What do you mean? Is something wrong with the roads?" I reply, annoyed that he had been calling me for the past few weeks about every little issue. Sternly he replies, "Mr. Hale you need to have someone clear those roads before your new arrivals get in" He sighs before adding, "I know you're new to this, but your aunt left instructions for you to follow for a reason." I frown at his accusation. "Mr. Jenkins, I have been on the plower's schedule since last Tuesday. I can't control their speed or efficiency." I reply as I open the door to my truck.

After climbing in and turning on the truck, I connect to the wireless speakers and buckle up. "Mr. Hale, are you aware that your sign is down and covered in snow? It looks like a branch may have landed on it" I get a sinking feeling in my gut. "No sir, I did not. Thank you for informing me. I'll get on it right away." *Time definitely got away from me.* "You do that young man. Don't forget I'm dropping buy tomorrow with some fresh baked goods

18

for your guests" Mr. Jenkins hangs up before I can respond. Gripping the steering wheel, I lean my head back to ponder on what led me here. *This was a mistake. I'm not equipped to finish someone else's dream, especially someone that lied to my face for 34 years.* "You just wanted to find answers, now look at yourself. You're the proud owner of some old cabins and a run-down Inn." I grumble as I pull out of the parking lot.

"Incoming call from Mom" my truck announces. I tap the steering wheel without thinking twice. "Hey sweetie, how are you? I just saw the weather, is everything okay over there?" My mother's comforting voice fills the cab, the tension eases from my shoulders slightly. "Do you need us to send anything? You know your father has nothing better to do. I can send him." She whispers the last part and I chuckle. "Thanks, but I think I have everything under control. Everything is ready for our guests arrival and Kristian gets back tomorrow. I also have two people interviewing for the housekeeper position today." I say. She stays quiet for a moment. "You don't have to do this, you know that right? You don't owe Dana anything. You can find the answers you're looking for without keeping her business afloat." She sighs before adding, "I just don't want you to get hurt or buried in debt out of some chivalrous since of duty you have." I smile. *She always knows how I feel without me saying a word. I don't know why I bothered trying to hide it from her.*

I exhale slowly before replying, "I have everything under control so please don't worry. Again, Kristian will be back tomorrow. We spent most of our summers here and we are both licensed tradesmen. Speaking of tradesmen, how's dad doing?" I change the subject as I pull in behind a snow truck "Please be headed towards the cabins" I murmur. "What was that sweetie?" My mom's concerned voice floats through the speakers. "Nothing sorry, I was talking to myself" She then tells me how dad hates retirement and is bored out of his mind. "He doesn't like golf or sports. He doesn't really have any hobbies either, so he's driving me a little batty. He wants to take a trip down to New Orleans to visit family soon. I hope you bring a special lady to the holiday banquet this year." she adds and I laugh." I chuckle and we continue talking about how things are back home. She reminds me not to forget to wear the scarf she sent. "It will keep your beard from freezing. I love you, call us if you need anything." She adds before hanging up.

After what seems like only a few minutes, I slowly cross the open gates to 'The Retreat'. The entire area is covered in a thick blanket of snow. *I would have thought this was an old snow buried homestead had I not known what was under all the snow.* I pull in by the nearest building. The two-story bed and breakfast my late aunt Dana hoped to restore, loomed ominously against the backdrop of snow. I start unloading the truck as my mind drifts. *Dana had new plumbing and electrical installed throughout the main buildings six months ago. It's a shame she died before she could see it reopen.* I grab my gear and look around. After some renovations, I was finally able to reopen the Retreat. *Unfortunately, only a few cabins are ready to be rented out, so that left the B&B as my 'humble abode' for now.*

After I finish unloading the truck, I start preparing for tonight. *Two guests will be arriving this weekend, a painter and a freelancer. I can't remember who is coming first and who delayed their arrival.* I check the note I shoved in my jacket pocket this morning. 'First guest arriving Nov 13th at 8pm: Sabrina Eldwin, 30, freelancer from FL, staying until Dec 11th in 'Workers Refuge'. Add-ons: daily meals, guided hike w/chef prepared picnic...' *Workers Refuge, got it.* I shove the note back in my pocket and get to work.

I imagine myself in a chair giving an interview about opening the Retreat. *Am I excited to host my first guest? Surprisingly, yes, I am. Even with working 12 summers here, I didn't really interact with the people that stayed here. Was I afraid they would judge the place prematurely and leave before giving it or me a chance? Absolutely. I admit the place still needs a lot of work and right now you can't even see the roads. It could pass as a horror movie film location with minimal effort.* I grimace as I look around. *I'm glad the snow seems to have stopped for now.* "Continue from the B&B to the entrance, then on to the sign..." *This is going to take a while, I hope Ms. Eldwin is running late.* I look up towards the sky. *Make that very late. I would guess I have about an hour before it gets dark to clear my way to the cabin.*

30 minutes later

I am nowhere near done and the snow, now falling heavily, hasn't helped one bit. "Clear skies till the weekend huh? What's all this then?" I throw out my arms and grumble as I finally arrive at the tall mound the used to be my sign. I angrily thrust my shovel into the middle of snow pile. A loud metal "TING" rings out and I frown. *That doesn't sound like a wooden sign.* I start moving the shovel around the mound until I see something black. "I wipe my hands against the snow trying to uncover more of whatever it is. *That's a window!* I start to wipe faster, looking for the door. *If someone is in there, they've been in there for at least an hour!* I hear a voice inside, but I can't make out what they're saying. "Just hang on!" I yell but my voice is muffled by my mother's scarf. *There's the door!* I move to pry the door open, but it's frozen shut.

I tell them I'll be right back as I carefully walk back to my truck for my tools. *I can barely see.* After grabbing my tools, I return to frozen door and start chipping at the ice. I wipe the excess snow away and quickly work on the doorframe. I smash my finger and yell, right as I pop the ice off the door. Fearing that it could be a child, I ignore my finger and rip the door open. I jerk back as a steaming bag of what smelled like chili, is thrust in front of my face. A young woman screams at me to take her food and I stare at her in confusion.

CHAPTER FIVE

November 13th

~Sabrina~

I manage to keep still as I extend my offering, keeping my eyes shut so that I don't become hysterical. The snow hits my face as I patiently wait for my death. "No thank you. Would you like some help?" I open my eyes upon hearing a human's voice. *It's not a bear! He's dressed in various shades of brown, so it was an honest mistake.* I exhale in relief. "Yes, please! Here!" I thrust the MRE into his hands and scramble to put my boots on. He sniffs the bag and holds it away from him. "What is this?" he asks while giving it an odd look. "Chili mac" I reply as if were the most obvious thing in the world. I start throwing everything back in the backpack. "I run a B&B right over there if you need to call someone" he points behind his shoulder. *Was there a building over there this whole time?* I squint my eyes, searching for a building. *I can't see anything in this blizzard.* "Thank you so much. I thought it wasn't supposed to snow for a few more days" I add while shoving the flashlight in the bag. He chuckles and replies, "Same". I smile, glad that a local was also caught off guard by the snow.

After shoving everything back in, I snap the backpack closed. I look back at my suitcase and bite my lip. *How do I carry everything?* A gloved hand appears in front of me, as though I summoned a mage hand from my college days "I can help." I look up, and his brown eyes soften as I take his hand without hesitation. *Whoa, his hand is huge.* My eyes drift lower and he coughs. "I mean I can carry your suitcase ma'am" he says as he looks away. *Oh, of course that's what you meant.* I grimace. *I*

22

had not hesitated for a moment when his hand appeared. Actually, I pictured him carrying me out of this like we were in a cheesy romance novel. I frown and feel the disappointment rising. *What happened to being your own knightess? You don't even know what he looks like underneath his beanie and scarf.* He coughs, alerting me that I was lost in thought again. I stand, dropping his hand quickly. "Oh, thank you. Sorry about that. Thanks for the hand though" *Stop talking.* I close my eyes, internally screaming at myself again.

"The B&B is close, but it can be hard to see with all of this snow blowing around" he holds out the tail of his coat before adding, "You can hold onto my jacket since I won't be able to hear you well". He picks up his tool bag and my suitcase before turning towards wherever he pointed to over his shoulder. I sling the backpack over my coat and grab onto his jacket. *I wonder if he is touch-avoidant?* I make a mental note to give him extra space. *Or is he afraid of me? I must look like a mess in my slept-in make-up and unbrushed hoodie hair.* I feel the sting of the snow through my sweatpants and grimace. *Alex can never know about any of this.*

I trip and pull the man-bear's jacket. He quickly turns and makes a muffled sound as he catches me. *He feels so warm. Even though our layers I can feel his heat.* I can't help but lean into him as he holds me against himself effortlessly. I look up into his brown eyes and find myself holding my breath under his intense gaze. He steps back and releases me before continuing towards the building ahead. *Look at him go, as though he didn't almost snatch my soul with those eyes.* I grimace as I realize I have a crush on a pair of eyes. *If you keep this up, he is going to think you are trying to seduce him.* I bite my lip as images of what my seduction attempts would like fill my mind. *Sabrina, how can you need a cold shower in the middle of a blizzard?* After shaking my head to clear my dirty thoughts, I grab his tool bag and follow after the manbear. I grab the tail of his jacket again, grateful that he slowed down. *He must be at a foot taller than me, or he's wearing heels.* I giggle and look over the bulky form ahead of me. *It's hard to make anything out under those clothes. Especially with snow stinging my eyes every time I try to sneak a peek.* I imagine nice and naughty small versions of myself landing on my shoulders. *It's the universe reminding you that this vacation is for relaxing, not dating.* The nice version reminds me as the naughty one scoffs. *What's wrong with a little fun on the side? So long as everyone is interested in the same thing of course.* I imagine my mini me's shaking hands in agreement, and grin.

~Logan~

I trudge against the wind and snow towards the B&B, grimacing at my current situation. *Twice now I've had to turn away from those green eyes of hers. And her lips.* I grimace knowing I couldn't stop myself from staring at her pouty lips earlier. *I almost leaned down when she looked up at me earlier. Get it together Logan, don't scare the poor woman.* With my throat feeling tight again, I use my free hand to loosen my scarf. *Wait where is my tool bag?* I stop and look back to see the woman behind me carrying my tool bag. She smiles with those full, pouty, lips again and I grab the bag. I mutter a quick 'thanks' and sling it over my shoulder. I turn back toward the B&B, slowing my pace a little. *It would seem that I owe Mr. Jenkins an apology.* I frown at the turn of events as I come up to the porch stairs covered in snow.

~Sabrina~

The manbear kicks around the snow, clearing what looked like stairs to the building in front of me. *It looks like a two-story cabin with a giant porch.* I watch him work to clear a path up to the door. *I'm glad I decided to take a nap earlier instead of trying to walk two miles to my cabin. There's no way I would have made it.* The manbear walks back down to fetch me. *It probably looks like I don't know how to climb stairs based on how I zoned out for who knows how long.* He offers me his hand, and I take it slowly this time. *I want to make sure I'm not misreading things again.* We slowly walk to the door as though I was an elderly guest and he, my kind and considerate grandbaby.

I walk inside and for a moment, I think about my current situation. *I am alone in the mountains, in a stranger's house, with absolutely no way to protect myself.* As my eyes adjust to the lights turning on, I look at the walls lined with photos of smiling people. *How homey.* He lowers his scarf, "I need to go back and get the rest of my gear. The phone is on the wall over there and the bathroom door is beside it to your right" He is back out the door before I can even thank him. "What a trusting guy." *Or, he really is afraid of me and doesn't want to be alone with me.* After setting down my backpack, I take off my coat and hang it by the door. Not wanting to get snow everywhere, I take my shoes off as well. I look down the hallway lined with photos. *Some look like kids laughing and enjoying themselves, others look like adults just living for the moment. Everyone is having a good time though.* I smile, wishing I knew what it felt like to laugh like them.

The floors seem very old. They creak as I walk towards the phone on the wall. "I haven't seen a landline like this in years" I look around to see if there's a rotary phone too. *The furniture and wallpaper look at least 30 years old.* I call Alex, but she doesn't pick up. I left her a voicemail telling her I'm safe and that I found a charming B&B along the route that I'll be staying at for the night. *I hope he lets me stay here, that is.* The line instantly goes dead and the lights flicker. *Oh no. I've seen these movies.* I start to count my breaths as I look for a weapon. *In and out, slow and steady.* A branch snaps outside and I jump. I look outside to see there is still a blizzard going on. "Relax, everything is fine you are simply at the mercy of a stranger's kindness" I say to myself while looking around for a pan or candlestick.

The door opens and I jump back in surprise. The manbear drops his bag and raises his arms slowly. "Whoa, easy now. It's just me" he says calmly, as though he were calming a wild mustang. The nice mini me pops in to remind that I have invaded this poor man's life, not the other way around. I sigh at the situation. "Were you able to call someone?" He asks while putting away various things from his bag. "I left a message but then the line went dead. The lights also started to flicker" I hold my breath as he removes his hat, freeing his shoulder length dark hair. He removes his scarf next, and I admire my savior all over again. *What a fine manbear you are indeed.* I take in the perfect amount of scruff on his face, accenting his jawline instead of hiding it. I drag my gaze away from his light brown lips back to his eyes, and his brows furrow. *I see he has caught me observing him.* Crinkling my nose in shame, I look away. "A tree might have fallen on the lines or could be the snow. I'm guessing you were headed to the ski resort up the mountain" He trails off as though he doesn't want the conversation to lead to me requesting a room. *Well duh Sabrina, you just spent a full minute checking him out.*

I smile and answer casually, "Actually, I was on my way to check into my cabin at the Retreat. The GPS said is about 2 miles from here, but I really don't think it would be safe to go back out there." His back stiffens and he looks at me. His intense eyes boring into mine. *Sir, if you keep that up I'm going to need to sit down.* "What did you say your name was? Your GPS is off a bit, it's not that far. I can probably take you to your cabin tonight." he says with a chuckle and I stiffen. *I don't want to risk sliding down the mountain in a blizzard.* "My name is Sabrina, I think it would be dangerous to drive in this weather. You said this was a Bed and Breakfast, right? Could I stay here tonight? I have cash." I add while keeping the panic out of my voice. *Please let me stay.*

He frowns, "Ma'am I can take you to your cabin, it's really no trouble. I know the area like the back of my hand" he says with an easy smile that would melt me if I wasn't arguing for my life right now. I reply in a rushed voice "No. Please, no. I really don't think anyone should be on these roads, especially in a blizzard. Are there any spare rooms here I could stay in? I can pay extra, even if it's for just a couch to crash on for the night." I ask again as I walk closer to him. I look into his eyes "I promise I'm not a crazy mur-" *Stop talking Sabrina!* I clamp my mouth shut and smile awkwardly. He turns and walks to the other side of the room. *Great now he thinks I'm crazy. Can't blame him for kicking me out into the snow now.* I sigh and bend over to get my bags. "You can take the room over there." He points to a door across from me. "It has a separate entrance and an attached bathroom.

All doors in the house are lockable from the inside. I need to wash up, so I'll start dinner in 20 minutes." He says before quickly shutting the door behind him. I hear the lock turn and my shoulders drop. *Oh. He didn't even feel comfortable taking his coat off in front of me. He really is afraid of me, great work Sabrina.* I roll my eyes at myself and grab my stuff, grateful he's letting me stay.

I walk down the hall towards my room for the night and brace myself for the great unknown. I push the door a little harder than I intend to, and it hits the wall with a 'thud'. I look back to see if the manbear heard it, but his door stays closed. I walk into the room and notice empty walls covered with peeling wallpaper, well past yellowing at the edges. I plop my luggage on the iron bed frame positioned in the corner of the room. I'm relieved to see a new mattress leaning against the wall, still in its plastic wrapping. I walk over to the desk and it wobbles under my touch. *It needs a few updates, but it has a lot of charm. I wonder how old this place is and if anyone else is staying here.* I hum as I continue investigating my room for the night.

"Is he still doing renovations?" I try to open the top drawer of the dresser in search of bedding, but it's wedged shut. The rest of the drawers open easily, but are empty. I move on to look at the small fireplace in the corner. "This is beautiful" I say while looking at the stone masonry. The lights flicker again as I grab my toiletries bag and pajama pants. *I should change before the power goes out.* I make my way to the bathroom and turn around. "Brush, brush, where is my brush" pausing when I see my reflection in the mirror on the wall. "No wonder the poor guy all-but-ran from me after seeing me in the light" My mascara was smudged all over my eyes. *I look like a racoon that just got off of day shift.* I groan knowing that first impressions are everything, and I have effectively bombed this one. *Wait, did he even tell me his name?*

I change out of my clothes and into the oversized hoodie Alex bought me. *I feel like I'm in a cloud.* I wash my face as I try to remember the manbear's name. *I don't think he told me. Granted*

I did throw myself at him, so I can't really blame him. "Okay much better" I saw while walking over to the standing wardrobe. The first drawer had sketching materials while the second drawer had a sewing kit and a bag of buttons. The third drawer had a few random tools, but still no sheets. I look at myself in the mirror and move my long, wavy, black hair over my shoulder. "I should probably put pants on" I murmur as I pull the mirrored door of the wardrobe right off its hinges and onto the floor.

CHAPTER SIX

~Logan~

November 13th

Earlier

Logan could barely stop the laugh from escaping his lips while locking his door. Walking to the adjacent bathroom, he flicked the light switch and turned on the faucet. Letting his laughter out, he wiped the corners of his eyes. *She really thinks I would be afraid of a little thing like her. I put her in a room with its own exit and bathroom so **she** would feel comfortable. I told her about the locks to ease **her** mind.* With a hiss, I take the smashed MRE out of my inner coat pocket and throw it in the trash. *Glad it didn't burn me too badly. I didn't even realize I'd been hurt until I went back for my shovel.* I grimace as I look at the mark on my .

After turning on the shower, I strip quickly and let my mind drift as I stepped into the spray of the water. My thoughts were currently headed towards a certain feisty, raven haired, woman with the prettiest lips I'd ever seen. *I wanted to kiss those pink lips.* Groaning, I turn the blue knob more. *I need to cool down before going back out there.* I rub my face and shake my head, *Why are you acting like this? She is your guest, and she will be your guest for the next month. Why didn't you tell her she was already at the Retreat?* I finish my shower in a rush, deciding to tell her sooner rather than later. I quickly shove my toned legs into my jeans. *Probably should have dried off better.* I groan as I pull on a pair of socks, the fabric sticking to my skin making it unnecessarily difficult.

I freeze as I hear a scream come through the walls. Rushing

towards the guest room, I throw open the door, prepared to fight whatever had broken in. *Be it human or other.* I was unprepared to see Sabrina standing in the middle of the room surrounded by shards from a shattered mirror. My eyes trail down the oversized hoodie and land on the thin red lines trickling down her legs. "Give me a minute" I said while turning back towards the hall. *I knew I should have fixed that door when noticed it.* I grimace as I tossed on a pair of boots and grabbed a broom from the closet. I start to clear a path from the entrance of the room to Sabrina. "I am so sorry. I pulled harder than I meant to and it just popped off. I must have gotten stronger from shoveling snow earlier" She says while covering her face. I feel my lips twitch. "It had rusted hinges I meant to replace later on. This was my fault, not yours." I set the broom against the wall and ask if it's okay for me to pick her up.

She nods and I scoop her up, careful of her injuries. Her arms wrap around my neck as she makes a small squeaking sound. My lips twitch again as I try again to not laugh at the little gray mouse in my arms. One glance at her legs and the amusement fades. "I hope you were at least done with your shower" I hear her say weakly into my shoulder. *She is clearly embarrassed.* "I was. I have a medicine kit in the pantry" I reply as I carry her into the kitchen. I set her down on a barstool and walk over to the pantry. "Do you need any help?" She asked after I knocked some things over. "No, I found it" I reply while silently cursing my lack of organization. *I'll clean that up later.* I grab the supplies I need and step over the spilled boxes.

After setting the bandages and antiseptic cleaning spray on the bar, I kneel in front of Sabrina. I gently start cleaning her tiny wounds, being careful to get all of the shards out. After placing the princess themed Band-Aids on her leg, I look up to see her staring at the ceiling. I take a moment and look at her face. Her high cheekbones accent her long eyelashes. *Her eyes look blue in the center now.* "All done" I say as she slowly looks down at me and smiles. "These are so adorable!" she exclaims while poking around the edges of her band aids. "I really appreciate you doing all of this, I get queasy at the sight of blood" she says sheepishly, picking at invisible lint on her hoodie. I stand quickly, noticing her hoodie had risen up to her upper thigh. "I'll go put on a shirt and then clean up the guest room" I walk back to my room and throw on a gray t-shirt, grabbing the dustpan on the way back to the guest room.

After dumping the broken mirror pieces into the trash, I vacuum to make sure there are no shards left in the hardwood. I unwrap the mattress and toss it on the bed. Once I straighten the mattress, I move to adjust the bedframe. I step back and look around the room. I should get a rug and maybe a good reading chair for this room. I jump as a voice softly says, "I was looking for sheets when I she-hulked the door" Sabrina nods to the wardrobe in the corner. I frown, realizing another mistake I made. *What was she supposed to sleep on? The plastic?* "They are in the hall closet along with things you may want for the room. Feel free to take whatever else you need from there." I add as she points at the desk. "Thank you, oh could you move the desk by the window? The snow is so beautiful. I'd like to look out the window while I use my laptop." *That's a better spot anyway.* I nod. "I'm going to make dinner in a bit. If you want some, I just need to know of any allergies or avoidances." I say once I finish moving the desk. *The desk wobbles, didn't know about that.* "Honestly, I like everything. I also like to try new things, so make whatever you like" she says while looking through the window. She turns and looks at me with those green eyes that remind me of soft prairie grass. "Oh, that reminds me, what is your name?" I frown, feeling like the air had been sucked out of me. *Wow, you still didn't tell her your name. Best retreat owner, ever.* "Logan, Logan Hale. I'm so sorry for the late introduction." I growl in frustration at my own shortcomings, adding more to the list.

"Sabrina Eldwin, pleasure to meet you" She holds out her hand with a smile. I shake her hand and smile back. *It's so small.* I glance at her hand in mine before replying, "We might lose power, so we need to team up and do some prep work if that's alright?" I say, dropping her hand before moving to the refrigerator. "I need to get the fires going in the fireplaces, set out lanterns, cook dinner, and make coffee." I say in all seriousness as the lights flicker. "I can make coffee and maybe help with dinner, if it's simple" she says while biting her lip. The lights flicker again and I sigh, "There are cans and boxed goods in the pantry if you aren't a confident chef. Help yourself unless it has VIP written on it. Big bold letters, can't miss it" I add with a reassuring grin. I move to start working on the fireplace as she opens the cupboards. I cough and turn my head as her hoodie starts to rise with her movements. She looks down and blushes before rushing back to the guest room. I laugh and continue to set up the logs.

Well, that took longer than usual. After getting the fireplace in the living room going, I stand and stretch for a bit. *The coffee smells amazing.* I ask Sabrina if it's alright to place a bundle of wood and a lantern in her room. She walks out of the kitchen wearing a pair of dark gray pants under the oversized hoodie "Yes, thank you. What do you take in your coffee?" She replies after taking a swig from her cup. "I like a bit of caramel in mine and lining the rim." I answer while setting out lanterns and lighters in various areas of the room. "That's how Daddy likes it too" I hear her say as she walked back to the kitchen. *She must be close with her dad.* I place the wood bundle in her room and set the pamphlet on fireplace rules on the desk. *It's already 7pm.* I frown, realizing I still haven't told her that her cabin is a few feet, *not miles*, from here. *I don't think she recognized my name.*

I quickly finish up in the guest room and walk back to the kitchen. I freeze once I see bread and condiments set out on the bar. "Ta-da! A DIY sandwich bar!" She exclaims proudly while throwing her arms to the side like a gameshow model. I look around and see nothing else set out. She puts ketchup on a piece of bread and raises it to her mouth "Wait. Absolutely not." I grab a plate and hold it for her to drop the offensive item on. I place it on the bar and add some rice to the rice cooker in the corner. "When this beeps, can you turn it off please?" I ask and she nods in agreement. I open the refrigerator and set out

32

some shredded proteins. She watches me intently as I season and toss everything in a pan with some olive oil. I glance at her and ask "Can you hand me a tomato, garlic, the bag of carrots, and a hatch chili please?" She nods and sets some things on the counter. "I don't see any chilis" she says after a moment, the door of the refrigerator muffling her voice. "They're in the tin foil" I reply, chuckling when she looks over at me with a frown. "The silver wrapping paper." She nods and holds up a foiled oval, "This?" I laugh and shake my head. "No, that would be a potato. Look for grilled green peppers, they will have black marks on them." I move the pan slowly over the flame. I hear her move things around and I frown. "I need the bag that looks like Chinese takeout art." Her face lights up before turning back to the refrigerator. "Found them!" She exclaims, proudly holding up the foiled chillis.

Who doesn't know what tin foil is? I shake my head incredulously as she excitedly hands me the bag. "Do you know how to dice a tomato?" I ask nervously. She gives me an intense look. Her green eyes burning into me as I stir. *I can tell she is about to tell me something serious.* I set the pan down and turn towards her. "Sir, I can barely peel a banana." She says with disappointment sagging her shoulders. I start laughing and she frowns. "I'm serious. I have to chop them in half at home and even then, I cut them in half again to make them easier to peel" she says. I wipe a tear from the corner of my eye before asking, "Wait, like long ways or in the middle?" I make cutting gestures with my hands, as images of banana boats on bowls of yogurt fill my mind. *I could add that as a breakfast option.* She scoffs and explains her peeling process as I continue thinking of banana boats for breakfast.

"Why did you add butter if you already had oil in the pan?" She asks me after I finish chopping the ingredients. I toss them into the pan. "The oil keeps things from sticking; the butter is for flavor. You have to be careful though; at high heat, they don't like each other much" I grin as I grab another pan and put a little oil and butter into it. "Now I'll put the lid on it and show you what I mean" I place the pan on the higher flame. "It isn't doing anything" she frowns. I chuckle at her impatience and tell her to be patient. Once the oil starts spattering against the lid, she jumps. "That could hurt if the lid wasn't there." She says as I move the covered pan to an un lit burner. My lips twitch as I continue sautéing dinner, now that our experiment was over.

The rice cooker lets out a high pitch beep, letting everyone in the county know that our rice is done. Sabrina jumped at the sound but quickly recovered to go shut off the machine. She crinkles her nose at the machine, and I smile. "Can you pull out two rice bowls from the cabinet to your right?" I ask as she opens the left cabinet. "Your other right" I grin as she mumbles something incoherent under her breath. After a moment I add, "The bowls we want are wide rimmed, shallow bowls, with a blue and white-Yes those!" I exclaim as she sets the two bowls on the counter. She grins at me with pride as I give her a thumbs up. *She shouldn't be allowed in the kitchen unsupervised.*

Once the veggies are nice and caramelized, I turn off the stove and put the pan on a back burner. Turning, I grab the bowls and scoop a few spoonful's of rice into each bowl. Using the back of the spoon to rub small circles into the center of rice, I form a crater. I add big spoonful of the steaming mixture from the stove into the crater and round off the top. "Just add a Nasturtium blossom to the corner and it would be perfect" I murmur as Sabrina stares at the food, a little drool pooling in the corners of her mouth. "A what?" She asks, never taking her eyes off the bowl. I laugh and hand her a spoon "A Nasturtium blossom is an edible flower with a peppery taste to it. Go ahead and eat, I'm going to get us some waters." She is already on her third bite by the time I finish my sentence.

CHAPTER SEVEN

~Sabrina~

November 13th
7:30pm

What am I eating right now?! I bite my lip to keep my moan to myself as the flavors merge together in my mouth. *What is this delicious flavor?* Logan's shoulders stiffen and I worry that I was too loud. They relax as he turns with two bottles of water in his hand. "It's good right? The rice is filling and helps balance the flavors if you prefer to eat your food separately." He says with a smile, his brown eyes light up as I nod in agreement as I chew. *Geez Sabrina, finish chewing and talk to him.* I take another bite and close my eyes. *Don't just keep putting more food in!* I berate myself as he talks more about the meal. "I forgot I skipped lunch. This is amazing, are you a professional cook?" I ask him before I shovel more food into my mouth.

He chuckles and lowers his spoon. "A chef? I have a culinary arts degree that I do utilize here, but only until I hire someone else. My aunt left me this place. It's been a lot of work to fill in her shoes. I'm getting ready to re-open it since her passing." He says with an odd tone. I look around the kitchen, noticing the new appliances and worn countertops. "I've been updating it slowly; my main focus was on safety upgrades for all of the buildings and then installing new appliances. I've been slowly modernizing a few of the cabins" He adds before taking a bite. "It looks well loved. Is the B&B open yet?" I ask, realizing that we haven't discussed pay. He hesitates and says not quite. *This poor man rescued me when he was already dealing with so many issues. Here I am just breaking his furniture and eating his food for free. I*

35

rub my temples while thinking about how to make this situation right.

He sighs and explains, "Two of the cabins are ready for guest occupancy. This building isn't ready to house guests. I had planned on hosting shared meals here or delivering them to their cabin if they preferred private meals." He takes another bite as I frown. *I wonder if most of the places around here offer that service.* "I'm so sorry, how much do I owe you for the night? Oh, the meal and wardrobe too. Money is no issue-" I clamp my mouth shut, already in the middle of nervous chatter. *Please don't make me go back out there. I promise I won't touch you. I'll gladly pay you extra for the trouble.* I silently add. "The wardrobe was my mistake. I should have warned you about it or better yet, I should have fixed it earlier." He leans back and rubs the black scruff on his cheek. "As for the room and meal, technically you already paid for that. Though you were supposed to check into your cabin, the Workers Respite." He stands to take our dishes to the sink. *Wait. What?* I look around slowly. "You took out my sign with your car. I'm guessing the snow had already covered it by the time you got out to check." He adds with his back to me. I blink as I register his words. "So, this is part of the Retreat? The one I'm staying at for the next month?" I look around again, not recognizing anything from the photos on the website.

He notices my furrowed brows and says, "The B&B isn't open yet so the inside isn't pictured on the website, only the outside. The kitchenettes you saw online were from the two cabins that are available to guests" He starts wiping the counters as I exhale slowly. *So that's why he kept insisting that he could take me to my cabin earlier.* "Why didn't you tell me when you figured out I was your guest?" I ask incredulously as I cross my arms. "To be honest I meant to, but things kept coming up. Then it slipped my mind after your injury" He sighs while running his hand through his dark hair. I walk over to the coffee pot and refill my cup. *Regardless, I kept grabbing him, broke his furniture, had him doctor my childish self after breaking said furniture, oh and I broke his sign.* "I still insist on paying for the wardrobe and the sign.

36

Where is the mocha sauce?" I ask, relaxing slightly knowing I will be here for the next 30 days. *The website listed a fully stocked tea and coffee bar with all the dressings.* He walks over and reaches into the cabinet above me. *Why does he smell like marshmallows.* I inhale and smile, imagining a campfire and smores. I snap my eyes open. *Did I just sniff him, twice?* I slowly look up to see if he noticed. He looks back at me and the corners of his mouth twitch. *He noticed.*

I quickly look down and move to the side. "Did you want anything else? I have cinnamon, vanilla, caramel, and more toppings in the fridge." Logan says as he sets the mocha sauce onto the counter. *He isn't offering his marshmallows, so calm down.* I shake my head. "Nope, I'm all good with this" I reply as I squeeze a generous amount of mocha sauce into my coffee. "At least I won't have to go far to unpack" I murmur. He grins as he pulls out a container and a jar of cherries. *Oh, those are the 'aged in a dark yummy syrup' kind of cherries.* I bite my lip and look down at my mocha. He pours a cup of coffee and adds a bit of caramel. Turning, he slides the whipped cream and cherries to me. "I wonder who can make the best-looking coffee with whipped cream, caramel, mocha, and cherries. Winner pays for the wardrobe." He adds with a mischievous glint in his eyes.

"You're on" Grateful that he wants a distraction too, I grin at him. I grab a spoon and put a nice sized dollop onto my coffee. I glance over as he adds small blobs to his. *I have seen countless foam art from getting coffees over the years, I got this.* After I form my mini mountain, I drizzle mocha and caramel on top in a zigzag pattern. We work in silence, intensely focused as the fire crackles behind us. I add a cherry on top and clap my hands "Done!" I turn and see mocha sauce covering some of the whipped cream blobs on Logan's coffee. I grin. *I am victorious.* "Nice mountain" he says with a smile. "Thank you. Nice, uhm…" I trail off, not knowing exactly what it is he tried to make. "Oh, whoops its upside down. Here it looks better next to yours" He turns the cup gently and places it next to mine. *Is that a panda climbing my mountain?* "Whoa. How did you do that?" I lean down and look closer, amazed at the detail. "How did you shade it and why does it look like it is about to climb out of your cup and onto my mountain?" I continue asking him more questions before he can answer the first one.

Logan smirks before popping a cherry in his mouth, "I told you, I went to a culinary arts institute. Should I offer coffee art as a class here?" He laughs while holding up a toothpick and I realize that I never stood a chance. After sipping on our coffees, we settle into light conversation about his plans for the Inn. "Once I am done renovating everything, it will be a huge success. The kitchen is perfect for two chefs, and we have several rooms in different sizes. Going from an Inn to a B&B shouldn't be too difficult." Logan continues explaining his vision for the cabins and some of the land. "So, what all do you do here? Do you have any other staff?" I ask while looking around. He exhales slowly, "I manage the Retreat as a whole. I'm a trained chef, licensed plumber, decent repairman, and I took a few night courses in business management at the local community college." He pauses to take a sip. "My partner will be arriving tomorrow to take over some of the maintenance work. He's a licensed electrician, decent repairman, excellent carpenter, and he has a degree in business." He points over his shoulder before adding, "We share that room over there. Once we hire more staff, we hope to offer lodging for them as well." *Oh, that kind of partner. Well, now I get why he was avoiding me so much.* I grimace as I think about my behavior earlier.

The lights flicker again, and I glance out the window. I see nothing but inky blackness against the white contrast of the snow built up in the corners of the windowpane. *It's oddly beautiful.* "A few people are interviewing tomorrow for the housekeeper positions. I had another housekeeper, but a few days ago she was put on bed rest for the rest of the month, possibly until she has her baby. She may not be able to come back until six to eight months from now. By then I'll need another housekeeper anyway, so it gives us both peace of mind on job security." I nod and drink the rest of my coffee. "My little cousin will probably move up he to help out with the groundskeeping. I've already placed ads for general maintenance technicians, cooks, and a few other positions." Logan shakes his head, some of his black hair falling loose against his forehead. "So far, it's been hard getting people to show up for an interview. What about you? Are you retreating from your troubles or making your troubles retreat?" He asks and raises his coffee to his lips.

I smile. "To be honest, most of my troubles are gone now. I'm on a journey of self-discovery, of sorts. A quest to find my happiness, if you will. Maybe I can learn some new things here and find discover hidden passions for something" I glance over to him and see his eyes darken at that last part. "I'm a man of many talents; I will teach you what I know" he says with a devilish smirk. *Yes please.* I move to take my cup to the sink, but he grabs it first. "You are a guest, regardless if you are in your cabin or mine" He leans down and whispers, "Don't worry about the dishes, that's part of my job." Logan walks to the sink, completely unaware of my blush. "What time is breakfast?" I ask him casually, already picturing what a trained chef could possibly make for breakfast. *Belgian waffles with honey butter and maple syrup? A breakfast quiche? Omelets?* My mind spins with all of the delicious images I can conjure.

"That depends on if the power is out, what time you want it, and if you want it hot or cold." He says over his shoulder. I bite my lip, unsure of what to say that will get me the most options to try out. "I don't have a preference, but I think I may try to sleep in. Maybe 9:30am?" He turns and wipes the counter, his brown eyes lock with mine, "Do you want me to wake you, or would you rather I make something that will keep if you sleep past 10am?" A vision flashes before my eyes. It's of me with my wavy black hair cascading down my back. I'm dressed in a purple flowing gown with Logan's muscled arms around my waist. He leans down as though to kiss me. *Yes, please manbear. Wake me with those big strong arms-* A cough jolts me as Logan asks me if ok. "You're turning red, are you sure?" I turn my head to hide my blush.

39

"I'm fine, but I should probably catch up on sleep. I don't really have any plans for tomorrow. No need to wake me." I reply hastily, not trusting myself alone in my room with him. "Sounds like you have plans to rest" He chuckles before adding, "I'll make something that will keep in the fridge so you can sleep as late as you like. That way if I'm busy with interviews, your breakfast will be ready regardless." He walks over to me as I nod. *I should get a purple dress.* My blush deepens at his closeness. He leans over to put something in the cabinet above me and I bite my lip. *This is the part where you kiss the sultry woman that has landed in your cabin on this snowy evening.* I tell him with my eyes. His eyes darken in response as he looks down at me. *Checkmate.*

He turns and walks into the living room to check on the fire. *Oh no.* I walk to my room quickly after completely misreading the moment. *Can you please behave? Do you want to end up outside with the real bears? He has a partner already!* "Have a good night" I say before closing the door. The firelight casts shadows around the room and I frown. *I probably should have looked around before shutting the door.* My eyes struggle to adjust to the dark as I shimmy my pants off. *I was so ready to go to bed, I forgot to grab the sheets.* I try to catch the pants as I kick them off. They land in a heap somewhere to my right and I sigh. I slowly feel along the wall for the light switch. My fingers feel the plastic, and I smile. "Yay!" I say in triumph as I tap the switch. I squint as light instantly fills the room, temporarily blinding me. "Oh no" I groan as the lights flicker off, staying off this time.

CHAPTER EIGHT

~Logan~
Two minutes ago

I frown as I hear the door close behind me. *I almost lost control.* I look down at the nail impressions on my palms. *Can I survive 30 days of this?* I toss a log on the fire and walk to the kitchen. The lights start to flicker. "And there goes the power" I say as the lights stay off. I rub a hand through my hair as the other searches for a lantern. *Good thing I set these out earlier.* The fireplace from the living room casts shadows across the kitchen. I feel for the edge of the coffeepot and grin. *Jackpot.* I grab the lantern and lighter by the coffeepot, lighting it as I hear the guest door crack open. "Hey Logan, can I borrow that when you're done?" Sabrina pokes her head outside of the room as she asks. "I left one for you on the counter in the bathroom. I can come light it and the fireplace now if you'd like?" I offer as I walk towards her. "Oh. Uhm, no that's okay. I think I can manage. I just need that one to light mine real quick" She replies nervously with her raven hair shining in the firelight, clearly fidgeting behind the door.

I smirk "Would you like borrow the lantern to find your pants and then I light the fireplace?" I ask, taking a gamble that she kicked 'em off the second she went in there. "Yes please" she says with a small voice, her hand reaching out for the lantern. I grin and hand it to her, "I put a few candles in the bathroom and on the dresser. I'll get some spare blankets and be back in a little while" She nods and closes the door as I turn back towards the kitchen. I light the candles along the way, creating a soft glow around the entire first floor. Once there is adequate lighting throughout, I grab some spare blankets. I walk by the couch,

41

draping one over the edge as I pass by. I knock On Sabrina's door and she opens the door with a smile. "Perfect timing." She says as she takes the blankets from my arms. I follow her inside and turn towards the bundle of wood stacked by the fireplace. "I'll just go brush my teeth" she rushes into the bathroom, and I squat down in front of the fireplace.

Once I get the fire going, I call Sabrina to show her the locks on the doors. "Thank you. I promise I'll read the fire safety pamphlet too." She grins at me as I tell her goodnight. I close her door behind me and exhale slowly. *That wasn't so bad. I can handle this.* I walk to the living room and look down at the couch. *Guess I'll be in here tonight to keep an eye on the fire.* I turn the couch into a makeshift bed for the evening. I pick up the notepad on the coffee table and start to make my list for tomorrow. 'Check the pipes, check the electrical box, make breakfast, shovel paths, check the cabins, conduct interviews, make lunch, dig out the car, fix the sign, catch up on tasks, make dinner.' I frown. *I need to move her to her cabin, but that depends on when she wakes up. Kristian may be able to handle that as well as give her a tour of the town.* The fire crackles as I continue planning out tomorrow, my eyes drooping as the night goes on.

Am I dreaming? I find myself floating amidst a dark fog. Bodiless voices fill my head, yet no words can be understood. "Hello? Is anyone there?" I call out against the fog and the voices go silent. "Do you remember the story?" A feminine voice says. "What story? Who are you?" I ask while looking around frantically for the woman who spoke. "You know... about the... mermaids." the voice replies in a broken voice. *Why does her voice sound like that?* "What are you talking about lady? This is the United Indigenous Territories of Colorado; we don't have mermaids or oceans here" I reply with a scoff. A skeletal hand grips my throat as the voice turns guttural "FIND IT!" I struggle against her grip as everything fades to black.

I jerk upright in the chilly air and blink a few times. at the fire, barely flickering in the fireplace. Rubbing my neck, I move to turn on the lamp. *The power's still out. What was that about?*

I rub my throat again, remembering the feel of the cold, boney fingers. *Why did it feel so real?* I look over to see the firelight dimly glowing under Sabrina's door. *She must have woke up and added some wood earlier.* I stand and walk over to the fireplace to rebuild the fire. *3:30am is too early to start chores.* I lay back down, resting my hands behind my head. My eyes close, unable to fight the lull of sleep anymore.

A few hours later I wake up to Kristian's knock on the kitchen door. I stand up and walk towards the kitchen. I look out the window and chuckle as I unlock the door. He walks in and grins, "I spilled water and froze my beard." He explains, already knowing my question. "I saw the smoke from the chimney in the guest room, is everything okay? I figured you'd be making breakfast by now." He adds while carrying various sized bags inside. "It's been a long night, let me change and I'll tell you about it. Keep it down though, our guest is still sleeping." I gesture over my shoulder as I take his bags and set them on the table. He grabs an apple and tosses me one. He leans forward before saying, "They are already done clearing the main roads and should be here within an hour or two. Did you get the email from our other guest, Mr. Pierson? He had to delay his arrival by a week." I frown and chew as he adds, "Which works out perfectly since a tree took out the stairs to Ms. Eldwin's cabin. We can swap their cabins." He takes a bite of his apple as I open the door and look out towards the guest cabins. Thick branches stick up from the snow-covered stairs. I lean my forehead against the door after closing it.

I groan, "At least it was just the stairs and not the actual cabin. We can't swap them; they had different requests. Mr. Pierson wanted peace and quiet to focus on his work, which is why he was placed towards the back. Ms. Eldwin wanted to be near a hot tub and be near the entrance. That way she could come and go easily to town or the hot tub. We have to fix those stairs today." I add before taking another bite. Kristian smiles, "We'll make it work. Luckily, we know the layout of this place with our eyes closed. Shouldn't take too long to dig out the sign and pathways. I'll go ahead and start on it while you work on breakfast for Ms. Eldwin." He grins and heads back out to finish unloading the truck while I change. *I still need to check for burst pipes,* groaning at the list that is ever growing.

Later

Once the truck is unloaded and the initial pathways are cleared; Kristian walks in and asks if Ms. Eldwin is up yet. "No, thankfully because the power is still out. I'm having to improvise a little." I reply while working on my DIY breakfast station. "There's sliced fruit, various spreads, yogurt, and some other prepped cold goods in the cooler. Don't worry, I think she will like everything." I assure him while placing the oranges in the basket on the counter. *I even made banana boats.* "They say it's looking like another snowstorm will be rolling in tonight. Where are the generators?" He asks with a frown, his gray eyes narrowing. "Their delivery was delayed and the only backups that worked are hooked up to the two guest cabins. I was really counting on that delivery yesterday. I'm telling you man, something weird has been going on lately" I look over at him as he finishes taking off his snow gear, his blonde hair disheveled from his beanie "Sounds like I shouldn't have went back home for the rest of my stuff yet. I told you it could have waited" he adds with a smirk.

I shake my head. "Grab a bagel and let's get to work on the stairs, it's almost seven. Oh, and we need to dig out Ms. Eldwin's car." I say while grabbing the bagel I had toasted on the gas stove earlier. "Wait, where's her car? I didn't even see a car out there" he replied while pulling the curtain back to look outside. "She knocked the sign over with it. That big pile isn't the sign my friend" I say after adding some cream cheese. I feel a pang on my chest where her bag of food burned me and I grin. "Alright what's with the cheesy smile? Start from the beginning, we can spare a few minutes" Kristian says while grabbing a bagel.

CHAPTER NINE

~Sabrina~

November 14th
9:20am

My body sways gently on a slow-moving river. My body feels weightless, my eyes feel too heavy to open. It's an odd yet peaceful feeling. *Now I feel like I'm on vacation.* I smile and blank my thoughts, opting to take full advantage of the moment. A soft voice fills my mind, "Help me." I struggle to open my eyes as webbed hand wraps around my ankle and pulls me under the water. "HELP ME!" The voice shrieks as something moves past me in the water. I flail my arms around, still unable to open my eyes. Feeling something hot coming towards my face, I throw up my arms to shield myself.

I open my eyes slowly, blinking as they adjust to the bright sun shining through the open curtains. *What was that?* I think about my dream and the unfamiliar voice. *Was I attacked by a mermaid?* I glance towards the fireplace; the fire died out a while ago it would seem. *That explains why it's so cold in here. The power must still be off.* The memories from the previous day continue to trickle into my mind. I roll over and throw the blanket over my head. *I did say I wanted to sleep in, so unless it's dark, I can keep sleeping.* Shivering, I snuggle deeper into the thick blanket, fully intent on sleeping until sunset if my body deems it necessary.

I sigh and roll over. Unable to go back to sleep, I get up and slide the curtains shut. Dust flies everywhere and I immediately start coughing. I wave my arms around to disperse the dust in the air, but it just makes it worse. *Well, I'm up now.* I continue to cough as I make my way to the bathroom, eager for a shower.

"Oh, that's right. I have no clothes." I looked down at my dark gray pants and black tee shirt. I think back on being caught pantsless twice last night and groan. I put my hair in a bun and grab my toiletries bag. *I should probably throw my contacts away, no need to hide my eye color anymore.* I think about how much attention my eyes got when I first started working at **the place that shan't be named**. *I should eat first and then dig out the Jeep. I need to go to town and get some clothes.* I start making a mental list of what I need to buy as I continue brushing my teeth.

After making the bed, I repack my suitcase for an easier move to my cabin. I check my phone and see there that I still have no service. *It's almost 10am, I could go shopping and be back in time for a late lunch if the roads are cleared.* I open the door and peek my head out in search of the manbear. After a quick scan, I make my way to the kitchen. *A DIY bagel station, that's cute. Looks like there are bagels, jams, nut butters, and a fruit basket. Better than what I would have made, but not as much variety as I would have guessed from a chef.* I pick up the note on the counter. "Ms. Eldwin, as of 9 this morning, the power is still out. We have already dug out your vehicle, but the roads are still being cleared. Lunch will be ready at 11am, and dinner will be at 5:30pm. We will discuss reimbursement for prepaid meals and lodging should the power remain off and you wish to relocate." My shoulders drop. *He wants me to leave? Of course he does, I basically threw myself at him on multiple occasions. He even dug out the Jeep to help me leave faster.* Frowning, I spread some multi fruit preserve on a bagel and take a bite. *I wish the power was back on so I could toast it.* I look down at the sad untoasted bagel in my hand as I chew the doughy bread. *I've got to fix things, I want more of the food he made last night.* I eat in silence, not noticing the cooler by the refrigerator .

After I finish eating. I grab my things and walk over to the front door. I stop to put my jacket on. *I'll just email him and tell him to refund the debit card I used to reserve my stay, minus the stuff I broke and the security deposit of course. No need for an awkward goodbye. I can find somewhere else to stay once I get into town.* I

46

bend over to put on my shoes, not hearing the door open behind me. "Oh good-" A deep voice says from behind me. I immediately turn, my body choosing to fight this intruder. Logans eyes widen in shock as my fist uppercuts his chin in true Superman fashion. "Oh no!" I yell as he stumbles backwards into another man's arms.

The blonde bearded man throws his arms out as Logan crumples. "Geezus!" he yells, barely catching Logan before he hits the ground. "I am so sorry! Are you okay? I didn't mean to hit you. You scared me!" I clamp my mouth shut before continuing my spiral. "Logan? Bro you good?" the bearded man shifts Logan as they slide down the wall together.

I grab my things and dart through the front door, slipping as I scurry along the freshly shoveled path. *You have to leave, now. Head straight for the airport, forget the refund you don't need it.* I groan and put my shades on. Upon reaching the Jeep, I unlock the door and climb in while tossing my bags in the back. "Come on, come on!" The engine sputters but won't start. I rest my head on the steering wheel and close my eyes. *There's no signal to call for a ride. I can try to walk to town, but I might get eaten or lost since the roads aren't fully plowed.* I exhale slowly as I weigh my options, lightly tapping my forehead on the steering wheel. *Do I really have to go back and ask the man I just assaulted, if I can please have a ride into town?* I smack my head against the steering wheel harder than I intend, as a knock against the window interrupts my thoughts.

"Ms. Eldwin? I'm Mr. Graham, the one helping Logan out here at the Retreat." The bearded man from earlier smiles at me from behind the window. "I need to pick up some things in town, would you like a ride? Logan is fine by the way, just a little embarrassed. He would have offered to take you, but he has to conduct a few interviews later." I nod and open the door, reaching back to grab my backpack and suitcase. Mr. Graham offers to take my bags, but I shake my head and decline. He frowns and walks ahead of me towards the big truck. *Why are you like this? Stop being rude.* I continue berating myself until

I bump into him. I slip backwards and brace myself for the hard ground, but two strong arms reach out and support me as though I weighed nothing. *Wait, didn't this happen earlier with the manbear?* I adjust my shades and thank him, I avoid his eyes as he hands me the bags I dropped.

Mr. Graham opens the door to his truck. I slip twice while climbing in and he asks, "Are you alright?" I buckle up as I feel my cheeks flush with embarrassment. "Yes. I just want to leave. Thank you again for the ride." I reply curtly while looking straight ahead. He looks at my luggage and nods. *I am mortified.* I look out the window as we start down the mountain. A black truck passes us as Mr. Graham says, "I apologize for everything that's happened. We completely understand if you want a full refund. I can take you to one of the most popular resorts on the mountain if you'd like. They have an excellent salon where I usually get my hair cut." He says lightheartedly. "Yes please, thank you." *And thanks for not pressing charges against me for assaulting your partner. Good thing I brought my bags with me.* I silently add. He turns up the heat and we continue the rest of the drive in awkward silence.

He pulls into the drop off area for 'Boulder Springs Inn' and assures me he will personally issue the refund by the end of the day. I nod and close the door after grabbing my bags. As I walk into the lobby, I'm greeted by smiling faces. "Welcome to Boulder Springs Lodge, are you checking in?" A woman who looks to be in her late 50s greets me with a check in book. I remove my shades and set my suitcase down. "Maybe, I'm hoping you have a room available for tonight" I say with a sheepish smile. She closes her book with a sad sigh. "I'm sorry young lady, but we are completely booked until February. You would be hard pressed to find any available lodging within 30 miles for the next few months." I frown as she continues to give me bad news, "They just announced all flights have been pushed or canceled due to the inclement weather over the next few days. If you are looking for a flight out, that might be an issue as well." I chew on my bottom lip as I process her words. *I'm stuck here with no where to stay?*

I shake my head, refusing to give up, "Do you have any clothing stores nearby?" *I should get some clothes and proper shoes while I figure out my next move.* "We have a few boutiques in house you can browse. Just take the second hall to your right and follow the signs" She smiles and turns to greet the family walking in behind me. I pull my suitcase along past the lobby. Various tribal artwork lines the walls with sculptures thoughtfully sitting in the corners. *This place is beautiful.* I look at the map of the Lodge on the wall and frown. *There are multiple boutiques, bakeries, gift shops, and even a salon in here. Maybe I can linger all night after all.* I smile and head towards the closest store.

After getting lost for a solid 15 minutes, I finally find one of the boutiques. *Granted, 5 of those minutes was spent confirming everything the woman in the lobby mentioned, thanks to the free Wi-Fi here.* A woman with long black hair smiles at me, "Welcome. Please leave your luggage at the baggage check to your right. Keep your number coupon with you since you'll need it to retrieve your luggage when you leave the store." I hand the attendant my bags, grateful they aren't asking for a room number. I put my coupon in my purse and walk towards the clothing area. *So many different things to choose from. Where do I start? PJs and dresses, and jeans and coats, oh my!* I clap my hands together softly, my mood completely turned around.

CHAPTER TEN

~Kristian~

10:45am

I sit down in the reclining chair towards the back of Wox's salon. He leans me back and places a steaming towel over my freshly shaved face. "Alright, now just relax under there and I'll be back to check on you shortly." I hear him walk away and I feel my shoulders relax. *I've been looking forward to a haircut and a hot shave all week. I was hoping to clear up things with Ms. Eldwin, but that didn't work out.* I frown. *We're lucky she isn't suing us.* I scowl and freeze as I hear muffled voices, "Right this way Ms. Eldwin. You're lucky we had a few cancelations." Wox says. A feminine voice murmurs something in reply. *Could it be the same woman?* "Everyone was so excited about the snow, the lodge was almost empty by mid-morning" I hear Wox exclaim.

I keep still and continue listening to him explain how popular the lodge is for skiing. "Yes, I noticed it was booked until next year. Everywhere else seems to be reserved or in use already too. I can't even get a flight out today because of the storm coming in tonight." I hear a deep sigh as they continue discussing her predicament. After a bit, Wox ask's her what she's looking to get. "I'd like your recommendation. It's been years since I cut my hair, I'm tired of it. If I'm going to be frozen in a blizzard, I should at least make a pretty ice sculpture, right?" I hear Ms. Eldwin reply and I frown. *Is she really stuck in Boulder Springs with nowhere else to stay?* "Oh, I know the perfect cut for you, but it's a bit drastic. I also know a place that has a cabin available. It's called the Retreat if I'm not mistaken." He adds while moving things. *Does he know?* I wonder what Wox is up to as she laughs, "I was staying there, but I think they kicked me out. It's a long story." He murmurs something to her, and she exhales slowly. "You know what? Surprise me. I don't even care anymore. I came here for a life change and I'm not leaving without changing something." Ms. Eldwin says dejectedly. I hear Wox gasp and clap his hands, "Oh, truly?" I guess she nods yes because I immediately hear furniture moving. "I had an idea for you the moment you walked into my shop, come honey let's get started. Let Wox work his magic".

"That's a cool name by the way, what does it mean?" She replies as he shakes out a cutting cape. "Thank you, it means Bear. Now, tell your hair therapist what's going on to cause such a need for change" *I should say something. Wox has completely forgotten about my existence.* I start to move but I'm stopped by the sound of sniffling. "Two weeks after turning thirty, I quit working for an abusive company that I wasted an entire decade on. I came here on my first vacation since I finished college to figure my life out, but maybe it's me. Maybe I'm the problem." Wox murmurs something to her before she says, "I literally assaulted the guy that rescued me yesterday. I ripped a mirrored door off it's hinges like I summoned my inner she-hulk. After that, I'm pretty sure I leaned in for a kiss and he ran away. Oh and I uppercut him like I was auditioning for Superman." Wox laughs and she huffs. "Now I have nowhere to stay with another blizzard hitting tomorrow" I hear her holding back her tears as Wox comforts her and tells her it is just bad luck. *This is a big misunderstanding; everything can be fixed! I need to talk to her.* I wait for the right opening to remove the towel and announce my presence. Wox clears his throat, "There could be some misunderstandings going on, how about we work on giving you a fresh look for now. I'm positive things will turn around **after** I work my magic." I get the hint and stay quiet. I hear soft music as He keeps the conversation light to avoid me over hearing anything personal.

Later

I had no idea getting a haircut was therapy for some people.

I think back to the forty-five minutes I spent mostly in silence with Wox during my appointment earlier. *I think we were all caught up in about five or ten minutes, I don't think he and Ms. Eldwin have stopped talking in the last twenty minutes. I'm not sure if they even paused to breathe.* Thankfully, I did learn there is no need to cancel her stay. I continue to think about our silly situation as Wox announces he is done. *Everyone is blaming themselves. We could be laughing about this over dinner tonight.* After they talk about how amazing her hair looks, she finally pays and heads to the in-house bakery at Wox's behest.

I yank the frigid towel off my face and stand slowly, stretching my stiff legs. "Tap and pay, we don't have all day" Wox says while appearing beside me with a grin. He holds out a mirror and black rectangle. I place my card on the rectangle and look into the mirror. My sandy blonde hair now cut short on the sides and a little longer on top. *I look like I'm about to start college again.* I rub my now smooth chin and thank him. "How did you know who she was?" I ask as we walk to the front of the salon. "Hun you were texting right in front of me as I cut your hair. I thought you were sharing some tea without wanting to be too public about it" I groan and he goes on. "I advised she go to the bakery on this floor first, to try their famous pies. I also told her about other shops, including one on the third floor that just got in some cute sweater dresses. Go fix it before it snowballs into an even bigger problem. Oh, and tell Logan I want him to visit soon, I know he's getting scruffy." Wox says quickly before waving goodbye. I head towards the bakery and look around for a woman in gray sweats carrying luggage around.

After checking both bakeries and two different shops, I head towards the last store in the building. I breathe a sigh of relief as I see multiple raven-haired people shopping. *Please be one of them.* I smile at the attendant and start walking around the store slowly. I shift various articles of clothing on the racks as I subtly check each person in search of Ms. Eldwin. *She isn't here, maybe she was able to find somewhere else to stay after all.* I sigh and turn back to the entrance as I hear a gasp from the dressing room

52

behind me. "Kris?" a feminine voice calls out. I whip my head around to see someone I never thought I'd see again. "Bri?" I say shocked as I look into the crystal blue eyes that captivated my entire being over a decade ago.

CHAPTER ELEVEN

~Logan~
Earlier

I blink slowly as Kristian lightly shakes me. "Logan, let's go man. You're not dead, shake it off" I look around and realize I'm on the floor, leaning against Kristian. "What did you do?" he asks while helping me sit up. "I think I scared her by accident" *And she reacted accordingly.* I rub my sore jaw thinking back to all the times I'd seen my dad scare my mom. *She always swung first too.* I smile and Kristian shakes his head. "You need to get ready and I'll go talk to Ms. Eldwin. I'll offer to take her to lunch in town, my treat. We can do the tour while we're there. Just sit still for a bit so you don't fall." He says while standing. I grab the bottom of his coat and say, "If she wants to leave, she's entitled to a full refund. We haven't exactly provided 'the relaxing retreat' as advertised". He nods and walks out, closing the door behind him. Leaning my head back, I think on what to do next. *What a mess. I still need to conduct interviews later and finish fixing the steps. Mr. Jenkins will be here soon too, I need to double check the paths so he doesn't slip.* I groan and brace my hands against the wall, fighting off the headache from the barrage of 'to-do's' currently flowing through my mind.

I stand up slowly and walk to the kitchen to get a glass of water. *The door to the guest room is open.* I walk over to check the fireplace. *Safety first, can't add a fire on top of everything else.* Thankfully it seemed she read the pamphlet and properly settled everything before leaving. I take in the neat room with no personal items or suitcase in sight. *Yea, she's not coming back.* A knock on the front door snaps me from my thoughts and I walk over to open the front door. "Mr. Hale you need to clean up

54

your pathways! I almost died out there." I take the towel covered basket of baked goods from Mr. Jenkins as he steps inside and flicks the light switch. "Why is the power still off? The rest of the town has power. Did you check your box?" He asks with a frown. I set the basket on the counter and answer. "Yes, I checked last night and again this morning."

He furrows his long gray eyebrows at me, "You probably don't even know where everything is. I'll go handle the fuse box while you try a muffin." He responds gruffly" I frown and he continues, "There's around 2 dozen and 4 different kinds. Baked 'em myself this morning. I'm trying some new recipes, so let me know what you think. Be sure to save some for your guests" He walks out the door before I can argue. The smell of the muffins distracts me from being angry. I grab one before quickly draping the towel back over them. *Lemon poppy seed. I haven't had this in years.* I take a bite and close my eyes. Enjoying the quiet moment, I feel the tension in my shoulders lift. *I really should have these delivered bi-weekly.* I think to myself as I take another bite, unaware of time passing by.

The lights turn on as I swallow the last bite. It feels as though I am being pulled back from whatever realm I was lulled to by the magic muffin. The kitchen door opens, and Mr. Jenkins walks through, grumbling under his breath, "Told you it was the box, it's always the box." I grin at him earnestly before shaking his hand, "Thank you kindly Mr. Jenkins. You saved the day, also I may have a new favorite muffin now. You've still got it" I add. He frowns at me before replying, "No one thought I *lost it* to begin with. When you were knee height, lemon poppy seed was your favorite. Your aunt always had me whip up a batch before you'd visit." He hands me a box and tells me to set it on the mantle. "It has different herbs and stones to help purify negativity and grudges. Thought you might need it" I thank him and place it on the mantle.

I'll take all the good luck I can get. I look at the wood carvings on the box as he walks to the door. "Well, it's getting to be that time again, I'll head on out." he says while opening the door.

"What time again?" I ask, confusion lacing my voice. "Lunch time kiddo, and save some pastries for the guests!" He shuts the door as I look at my watch, "10:45? How did I lose an hour?" I notice I have a missed call from Kristian and check my voicemail. *He said not to worry about lunch, but didn't mention anything about the situation with Ms. Eldwin.* I walk to my bedroom to change before the applicants arrive. *I can only afford to hire one housekeeper for now, especially if Sabrina cancels her stay.* I rub the scruff on my cheek with the back of my hand. I contemplate shaving it, but the thought of snow hitting my bare face every day quickly changes my mind.

Once I'm ready, I walk over to the desk and pick up the two applications Kristian left on my desk. "Willow Hawthorne, 26 years old, has experience in housekeeping, cooking, bookkeeping, lawncare, pool and hot tub cleaning, as well as light secretarial experience." *Well, she sounds perfect.* I look over the rest of her resume, ready to hire her on the spot until I see the note at the bottom. "Jointly applying with Lunabella Hawthorne. What does that mean?" I pick up the second application, "Lunabella Hawthorne, 22 years old, has experience in housekeeping and accounting. Jointly applying with Willow Hawthorne." *We may have to hire more help if we don't want to screw up with the next guest too.* I lean back in my chair and close my eyes as I try to think of solutions.

"Hello?" a feminine voice says from outside. I look up to see a smiling blonde wearing white earmuffs decorated with light pink snowflakes. She waves eagerly to me from the window and I stand. I walk to the door, embarrassed for being so lost in thought. "Sorry about that, I didn't hear the knock" I open the door and look down at the two women standing in the doorway. "That's alright, I get so into my work that I disassociate too. Sometimes it's a coping mechanism, do you have any hobbies? Those can help a lot." The young woman wearing the earmuffs replies excitedly. *She has a lot of energy.* I smile as the other woman shifts, "Luna, slow down. We are here for a job interview, remember?" The brunette says softly. Her brown eyes lock with mine as she introduces herself. "My name is Willow Hawthorne, and this is my younger sister, Lunabella. We are here for the housekeeping positions. I believe we spoke with Mr. Graham a few days ago" she adds.

"Yes, Kristian Graham is my partner here at the Retreat, I'm Logan Hale." I open the door wider and step to the side. "Please come in. We can discuss everything at the dining table." I smile as they walk in, Lunabella's eyes widening as her eyes adjust to the darker entryway. "Would you like anything to drink? I have water, tea, coffee, oh and some fresh pastries made by a local baker." I offer as I lead them to the dining table. "Yes please. I would like a mocha with whipped cream and what kind of pastries do you have?" Lunabella asks excitedly while looking at the towel covered basket. I chuckle as her sister whispers something to her. "But he asked, and I do want a mocha with whipped cream and a fresh pastry." Lunabella replies honestly as her sister starts to apologize on her behalf. I hold up my hand, "Ms. Lunabella that sounds like an excellent idea. I've had a stressful morning." I pull out two mugs and set them on the counter. "Last night I had a caramel coffee with whipped cream, and it cheered me right up." I smile at them as Willow frowns, but doesn't comment. "Help yourself to something in the basket while I make coffee. You want one too?" I ask Willow while holding up another mug. She nods no, but Lunabella nods yes franticly behind her. "I'll make an extra just in case." I grin as I grab a mug with a tree painted on it.

"So, explain what you ladies meant by jointly applying with each other. I have several positions available, but I may can only hire one housekeeper at this time." I ask while setting up the French press. "Mr. Hale, I have a lot of experience in various positions. I have no issue filling in for multiple positions at minimum wage, so long as my sister is hired as well." Willow continues to list her work experience over the past 10 years. "That's an impressive resume. You started working at your aunt's motel after losing your parents in an accident when you were 16 and Ms. Lunabella was only 12." I frown and offer my condolences. Willow smiles and replies "It was a long time ago and we weren't that close. My aunt retired and sold the motel a few years ago. We have gone wherever jobs are available since then." *They seem perfect, but how can we afford both of them if Sabrina cancels?* After I pour the coffees, we dress them and sit at the table.

"I'll be honest, I can only afford one of you right now. That's not to say I won't be able to hire more later on." I add quickly as Lunabella starts fidgeting. "Originally, we advertised for two or three housekeepers, but we just had an unexpected setback. We're having to make a few adjustments. I don't want to hire you and then have to let you go after a week or two if the next guest cancels." I say sadly. "If you have a spare room, I can work for that as my pay. It doesn't have to be just housekeeping. I know how to fix things and can learn any trade if taught." Lunabella says while looking at the floor. Her sister looks at me and nods in agreement. "Yes, we are very flexible and have no problem working out some sort of arrangement." Willow adds while looking at me with a determined edge to her voice.

"We have plenty of rooms upstairs, but all of them need repairs. Wait, let me think." I close my eyes and rub the bridge of my nose. *They could stay in the private room Sabrina used until I can fix the rooms upstairs.* After a moment "I have one room that might work for that. It's the room right over there" I say while pointing to the room Ms. Eldwin stayed in last night. "It only has one bed for now, but it does have its own entrance and bathroom. Feel free to take a look. The room that I planned for staff to stay in isn't ready yet." *I also wasn't planning to offer lodging until after a probationary period.* Willow smiles, "Luna, why don't you look at the room, while I sort out the details with Mr. Hale?" Lunabella nods in agreement, "Okay." Willow turns to face me with a pleading look in her eyes.

"I'll be blunt Mr. Hale; I need this job. Luna's more trusting of people than she should be. I need to make sure she is safe too" I frown as she walks over to the sink. "We have no family or friends, so you don't have to worry about us asking for many days off. Since we only have each other, we love working holidays and staying busy." She faces me after setting her and Luna's mug in the sink. and her eyes soften. "If you can only to hire one of us, I would prefer room and board as payment and my sister allowed to stay here with me." I glance through the window. *Where is their vehicle?* "We got a shuttle from the motel." She adds as though she read my mind. I furrow my brows and nod for her to explain. "We moved here last week for work, but the job we had lined up fell through." *A risky move, but it seems like they didn't have much to lose already.* She looks towards the open door to the guest room. "Since the tickets were non-refundable and we had already sold mt car, here we are." She adds dejectedly while watching her sister inspect the bed frame in the guest room.

They need this too. I should call Kristian and get his advice. "Can either of you cook?" I finally ask after weighing my options. "I have been cooking for my sister and I since I was 11 years old. I'm neither great nor professionally trained, but there hasn't been a recipe I haven't been able to learn so far." She looks to see if her sister is watching and whispers, "Luna shouldn't cook. Ever." She looks me straight in the eyes and shakes her head firmly. *What horrors did her sister make her taste?* I shake my head, imagining when Sabrina almost ate a ketchup sandwich. "Let me make a phone call. Would you mind waiting in the other room with your sister?" She nods and walks into the guest room. I can hear Lunabella go over every detail of the room, and list out all the repairs she could make. I chuckle and type in Kristians number on my phone. I hold back my laugh as Lunabella further explains how to fix the stuck drawers and wobbly desk. *She could be very helpful too.* I smile, hoping for the best as the line rings.

59

CHAPTER TWELVE

~Sabrina~
Earlier

What am I going to do? I can't just go from shop to shop until tomorrow. I groan as I flip through the same clothes rack for what feels like the hundredth time. "Oh wait! I didn't see this earlier" I pull out a black sweater dress that feels like a soft blanket. *Maybe they have it in purple too.* I walk to the dressing room with my prize. After putting it on, I rub my cashmere clothed arms and sigh. *Why does it feel so soft? It's like my skin is being hugged by clouds. I must have this.* I gawk at the price and remind myself I deserve this soft, huggy dress. I look in the mirror and jump at my reflection. The messy long hair that was trapped in the messy bun earlier, now hangs loose in soft waves, cut just above my shoulders. My blue eyes almost look like crystals with my hair framing my face. *Glad I decided to throw my green contacts away this morning.* I press the attendant button and request the same dress in whatever other colors are available.

After a few moments, an attendant brings a small rack of dresses in mauve, pastel pink, dark purple, burnt orange, chocolate brown, deep red, navy blue, and baby blue. She smiles and walks back to the front. *There is no reason to get them all.* I slide the baby blue dress on and groan at how my eyes literally sparkle while wearing it. *I must have them all, there is no reason to even try them on at this point.* I grin and decide to try the purple one on anyway. *It's been so long since I felt free to be myself and wear whatever I want. Granted, I may be sleeping in a changing room tonight, but I'll look great doing it.* I laugh as I try to focus on the positive. *I didn't bring any dresses with me, and these would suit any occasion.* I smile as I decide to get them all.

I poke my head out to ask if there are any matching coats. I freeze once I see a tall blonde man with broad shoulders standing amongst the racks. *Oh, hello.* He turns his head and I see a chiseled jawline that I could never forget. *What is he doing here?* "Kris?" I ask, gasping as his head turns towards mine. His soft gray eyes lock onto me and I'm unable to stop the smile forming on my face. "Bri?" He replies with a shocked expression. He pauses for a moment before walking towards me. "You look amazing, have you changed at all?" he adds while looking me over. I laugh and reply "I guess it doesn't look it but yes, this is actually new" I gesture over my entire body as he laughs. "I haven't seen you in what? Over a decade? How've you been?" He asks as I grimace, "Decade? It hasn't been that long, has it? It's a long story, are you staying in town or?" *I hope he knows somewhere that has availability. Or a guest house. I remember his family had a guest house in the mountains!* I smile and pick a piece of invisible lint off my sleeve.

Kris smiles back, "I'm helping a buddy out with his place right now; this is my hometown. What about you? Are you in town for long?" He asks while looking at me, oblivious to the other women staring at him. *He always did make me feel like I was the only one in the room with him.* Suddenly, memories from long ago fill my mind. *Us under the stars in a tent, embraced in each other's arms. Good times.* I shake my head and lean against the opening of the dressing room. "I'm actually looking for a place to stay, all the Inns are booked" I say, opening the curtain more so he can see how I've *grown* over the past decade. His eyes darken. *Oh yes Sabrina, throw yourself at him. Daddy would be so proud.*

I flutter my lashes at him as I summon my inner temptress. His gaze drops lower and phone rings, cutting him off before he can reply. "I'm sorry, I need to take this." He says with a pained expression, "Hey Logan, how are the interviews going?" He turns around and I feel the air leave my lungs in a rush. *No way. There is absolutely no way he is talking to the manbear.* I look at him again and notice that he is wearing the same clothes as Mr. Graham. *Kristian Graham. He told me his real name back then.*

I grab the door frame to steady myself. *I sat next to him the whole way into town?* He continues his conversation, completely unaware of my mental spiral. "No, I haven't found her yet. I'm telling you, this whole thing has been a big misunderstanding. You think she's mad at you, she thinks you're mad at her, it's ridiculous. Ya'll are like an old married couple. Now she is wandering around with no place to stay and-" I tug on Kris's sleeve and he looks down at me. "I'm your guest, Sabrina Eldwin. I think we rode here together" I say softly while biting my lip.

His eyes widen in confusion as he registers my words. He clears his throat before saying "Go ahead and hire them both. I'll sort everything out here and we'll be back in time for dinner. Text me whatever you need in town." He hangs up and exhales slowly. "You really meant everything was new, including your last name." He says after looking me over again, this time slowly, and focusing more on my empty ring finger. "Hey! You got a glow up too, and I'm not married. I lied about my last name back then" I say nervously. He sighs, "Understandable. Let me explain the misunderstanding between you and Logan while we grab some lunch, my treat" He adds with his most charming smile. "That would be great, but I assaulted your friend. How is that a misunderstanding?" I ask incredulously. "That's... Not how he explained it." He goes on to tell me what Logan told him from his point of view.

Once I change back into my sweats, we walk towards the front together. "So you see, no one is actually upset with anyone. We all want the same thing, for you to have a pleasant stay at the Retreat" Kris grins while pushing my rack of dresses for me. I laugh as we walk up to the checkout counter. "How silly are we?" I ask as the assistant scans my clothes. He shakes his head and replies, "Very. Logan will get a kick out of this when we get back." I hand my coupon for my luggage to the cashier as she stares at Kris. "This is where your luggage was hiding" he murmurs while taking my bags. "Now that you know it's me, I can't carry my bags?" I ask while shoving his shoulder lightly. He leans down and says low, "I only let you carry them earlier because I thought you were going to sue us." I crinkle my nose as the cashier says the total out loud. I smile and hand her my debit card. *A knightess needs proper armor after all.*

I open the door to the parking lot as he carries my luggage and dresses awkwardly. "I can carry my things Kris" He grins and continues leading me to his truck. "Sir you never had to work hard for my attention" I say under my breath. I hear him inhale sharply. His eyes darting to mine with his nostrils flaring. *I know that look. He definitely heard me.* I chew my bottom lip and walk up to his truck, recognizing it from earlier. I watch as he unlocks my door and sets my luggage and bags in the back seat. "My lady" He says with a slight bow, never taking his eyes off mine. "My lord" I curtsy and climb in. I feel my face getting hot as I remember the last time he bowed to me. *I was wrapped in your black silk sheets in your tent. I captured you and told you glamping wasn't allowed during LARP sessions. After that night, I glamped with you for weeks.* I turn towards the window to hide my blush.

"Bri, are you alright? You're fully entitled to a refund to stay wherever you want. I'll help you however I can." He says while focusing on the road. I answer, "No, nothing like that. I was just lost in thought, that's all. Also, I go by Sabrina now" *I was only thinking about one of the last times I saw you and we just so happened to be naked. Like most of the times I saw you. I think this may be the most clothed I've ever seen you.* I turn back towards the window as he chuckles. *He knows.* I groan and rest my forehead against the window. "I see. Well then, *Sabrina,* is there anywhere else you need to go before we eat, or do you plan to wear a dress morning, noon, and night? We will need to be back by 4pm in case the snow drops early again." He laughs as I look at him. "I had already gotten some outfits from the same store you found me in. I had gone back in case I missed something. I'm glad I did because I almost missed the best dress in the whole Lodge." I reply with a laugh.

"By the way, was that an Inn or a Lodge? I saw signs for both." I ask while looking at the snow-covered mountains. "Technically both, and more. It's jointly owned by the local tribes and each area, or store, is ran by its own tribe. Boulder Springs is part of the UITC, United Indigenous Territories of Colorado." He adds after noticing my confusion. "The Inun-ina, Nuu-ciu, Ka'igwu, and Numunuu are the main leaders on the council for the UITC. Most of the main businesses involving land or tourism, like the one back there, are jointly owned with each tribe's culture being celebrated individually. The Nuu-ciu own Wox's salon and a few other shops, but the Ka'igwu own the main Lodge and bakery. On the other end you have the Inn and spa which is owned by the Numunuu. The Inun-ina run the outdoor festivities and the ski resort. There's more to it but that's all I know." I nod and then turn towards him. "Did Wox cut your hair too?" I ask as the corners of his mouth lower slightly.

He sighs, "Yes. I was in the back with the towel over my face. I wasn't trying to eavesdrop though. I had just gotten a haircut and hot shave. I'm glad I stayed. If I hadn't been there, I wouldn't have found out this was all a big misunderstanding. I also wouldn't have found you again." He says the last part so low I almost didn't hear him. My heart flutters and I pat his hand, grateful he stayed too. My naughty mini me pops up and reminds me that grown women deserve some relaxation. *He was clearly interested before the manbear called. What better way to relax than with a man that already knows how to make you-* Kris clears his throat and I realize my hand had traveled over his hand and onto his thigh.

I jerk my band back and apologize. *Please earth, swallow me now, or at least these wandering hands.* "Are you staying at the B&B?" I ask as he focuses on the road. "I share a room with Logan. I was visiting family for the last week or so" he adds. "Okay now I'm confused. I thought Logan and you were a couple?" I ask and he laughs. "We are both single and partners only in regards to the Retreat, not the bedroom." He laughs again and I remind myself there have been several misunderstandings lately, what's one more? "We are still fixing up the rooms at the B&B and Logan is conducting interviews now." He smiles at me before going into deeper detail about his goals for the B&B.

After a while he pauses. *I enjoy how passionate he is about this.* "Does Logan feel the same?" I ask as he turns into a parking lot. "Logan's had a rough year. Ever since we were kids, we wanted to buy this place from his aunt and renovate it. When she died and left it to him, he was hit real quick with the financial aspects of running a big place like this. She left him a lot of money for repairs, but there have been setbacks" he replied honestly. "You already know my situation from eavesdropping at the salon. Explain it as though I were contemplating being an investor" I say while laughing at his frown.

He glances at me while waiting on a parking spot and asks, "Are you serious Bri?" I nod and he continues. "The hiking trails, bridges, pathways, and lodgings have to be maintained professionally and inspected weekly. The roofs for all buildings needed replacing, which was the first thing Logan knocked out. Most of the cabins haven't been updated since the early 90s." *I hope he means 1990s.* "sounds like a lot of work" I say as I hold my wandering hand. *No more sympathy from either of you.* I mentally scold my hands as he replies, "All of the safety related tasks were handled first, then we conducted upgrades based on priority." He turns off the truck and leans back in his seat. "Realistically, we should have waited another month before opening. We could have done a little more to prepare. The generators are straight up MIA at this point. Logan swears his luck has turned sour, so Jensen and I are determined to turn it back for him." He says with a determined grin.

CHAPTER THIRTEEN

~Logan~
Earlier

Kristian hangs up after assuring me that everything was alright. *He said he and Ms. Eldwin would be back for dinner.* I walk into the guest room as the women turn to face me "Looks like everything's working out after all. If you and your sister don't mind sharing this room, you both can stay here and start work either today or tomorrow." Ms. Lunabella starts rubbing her fingertips together and smiles as her sister requests to start now. "If you two can handle the housekeeping, meal prep, sweeping the porch, and cleaning; we will provide lodging, daily meals, and cover utilities with a starting monthly salary of $1,500 each, after taxes. You'll be free to use the amenities provided here at no cost to either of you. There will be a one-month probationary period to make sure everyone works well together. Does this seem like something that could work?" Willow glances at her sister and nods.

I smile reassuringly at them and add "Once the probationary period ends, you both will sit down with us, and we will negotiate a 6-12 month contract with an increase in pay. If this works for you and Ms. Lunabella, I'll draw up the paperwork while you call a taxi to go get your things. Keep in mind your room will change once renovations upstairs are done and you may end up in a smaller room." I add, wanting them to make well-informed decisions. "Will we have the option to work here forever or is it just for one year?" Lunabella asks while looking around. I laugh and tell her it depends on how everything goes, but we would love long term staff. "Ms. Hawthorne, would you mind filling out these forms before you go?" I ask while handing her the employment tax forms.

"Yes. Thank you so much Mr. Hale, you won't regret this, I promise. Please call me Willow" Willow says, her voice heavy with emotion as Lunabella walks out the front door. I sit down at the desk as she fills out the paperwork. The door opens after a few moments, and Lunabella walks in with two suitcases. Willow smiles sheepishly and explains that they had brought their luggage with them and left it on the porch during the interview. The motel they were staying at was booked, so they couldn't extend their stay there. My gut clenches as I imagine what could have happened if I hadn't hired them. Lunabella walks over, her hands fidgeting by her sides. "Thank you for letting us stay and work for you Mr. Hale. You may call me Luna since we are friends now." Lunabella says with a smile.

Willow walks over and leans towards Luna, "Luna, he is our boss, not our friend." Willow whispers and Luna's smile falls. "I'm sorry-" She starts to apologize but I raise my hand to stop her. "Call me Logan. My partner and I have a vision for this place. This isn't about money for us, although we would like to make enough to make ends meet at least. We want to create a place where not only guests can come to feel rejuvenated, but also a place where workers are treated like family. We want everyone to enjoy their time together, guests *and* staff." I add as I walk over to the hall closet to grab some blankets. "Until the decks are repaired in the rooms upstairs, no one will be staying in them. The laundry room is upstairs at the end of the hallway. We just got new washer and dryers. so if there are any issues, let me know." I smile as Luna slowly takes the blankets from me and nods. "Kristian said he and Ms. Eldwin would be back in time for dinner. I had planned a few personal pot pies, one of you can help me prep later. I also need a list of furniture you will need for your room upstairs. Please include measurements for the areas you want each item to go" I add as I look at the sisters in amusement.

Luna's hand was thrust into the air as soon as I asked for measurements. "I volunteer as trib-" Willow pushes Luna's hand downs as she interrupts her sister, "I have made many types of pot pies and I'm sure Luna agrees that she would be better with measurements. Luna why don't you go ahead and unpack, then start on making the list for Mr. Hale?" Willow smiles at her sister and pats her hand. "Yes, I would like that" Luna grabs their bags and takes them into the guest room. I set down a tape measure, legal pad, and a pencil for Luna to get later. "Mr. Hale is my father, by the way. Please call me Logan" I turn to add, "Tomorrow we can go to town to get what they have in stock and order what they don't." Willow turns and mentions the incoming weather, and I frown. *That's right. I still haven't finished checking everything. I may not have time to inspect the cabins by the falls.* I rub my beard covered chin as I think about everything I need to do.

"If you need us to help out with storm prep or any chores that need to get done before the storm hits, we are ready to start now. We can unpack later" Willow says determinedly. "I need to do a few light repairs and finish checking the guest cabins. Let me give you and Luna a tour before we do anything else" I smile reassuringly. "Sounds good, I'll go get her." Willow says while heading into their room. *Hopefully my luck will change. With their help, I should get everything finished before the storm hits.* I shrug my coat on as the sisters walk out and grab their coats. "The two guest cabins have generators already hooked up. Since one guest pushed their arrival to next week, I'll be moving their generator to the B&B in case we lose power. It's a smaller generator so it won't power everything, but it'll keep the perishables from spoiling." I add while following them to the front door.

Luna opens the door and says, "It would be better to move both generators to the B&B and have everyone stay in one building." I shake my head at Willow before she can answer. "I'm not sure if any of the rooms are able house guests yet. Some of the flooring needs to be replaced and the deck rails aren't supported. It's a safety issue." She frowns as we step onto the porch. "Willow and I could sleep in the living room tonight and keep watch over the fire. We will be up early to help with breakfast anyway." She adds while looking around. "I

68

have a few ideas, but I'll need to discuss it with my partner" I reply. I turn and point to the cabin closest to the B&B. "That will be Ms. Eldwin's cabin, she will be staying with us for the next month. She arrived yesterday during the storm and stayed in the room you saw earlier. We were fixing the stairs to her cabin this morning, so I haven't had a chance to check the inside thoroughly yet." I think back on when Kristian and I were rushing everywhere while checking for busted pipes. "After the tour, we will check the inside of the cabins. Afterwards, we can see what condition the rooms are in upstairs." I say while leading the women down the stairs to start the tour.

CHAPTER FOURTEEN

~Sabrina~
A few hours later

"This town is amazing. It has everything you could want" I say as I glance at the various shops and cafes lining the cobblestone path. "I can see why you moved back here" I add while smiling at Kristian. "Yea, the people here take care of each other. Logan and I grew up together, we worked at the retreat most of our summers. He offered half of the place to me if I stay and run it with him. I'm seriously considering it" He adds while opening the truck door. After setting the bags in the back he turns towards me asks, "Anything else?" I grin and look at all of the stuff packed into his truck "Do you even have any space left?" I laugh while asking. "I have the topper on; I can stack and strap if I need to" His gray eyes sparkle as he slaps the top of his truck. I shake my head and climb into the truck as his phone rings.

He climbs in and answers, "Hey Logan, what's up?" He mouth an apology to me and I nod as I pull out my phone. *I still need to apologize to the manbear. It's 2:30pm, we still have a few hours until dinner.* I think as I check for a signal for the hundredth time. *My chosen phone company doesn't seem to know this place even exists. Maybe I should swap carriers while I'm in town. Maybe something with worldwide coverage.* I look over and see Kris focused on his phone call, his smile dropping into a frown. "Yea that makes sense, let me write that down. Do you think we can get everything ready before the storm hits?" He asks Logan as I pull out the pen and miniature notebook I keep in my purse. He smiles and mouths 'thank you' while taking them. I nod and look at the smiling faces of the people walking down the street. *It's so peaceful.* I lean my head against the window and close my eyes.

My eyes snap open as I hear the truck turn on. "I didn't want to disturb you, but we need to make one more stop before we head back." I listen as Kris explains

the plan to have everyone stay at the B&B tonight. "I'm sorry Bri. I feel like I'm treating you like an old friend that can be shuffled around, instead of someone who paid to be pampered on vacation" He grimaces as though he hasn't been pampering me for the past few hours. "Kris, you took me out to eat at an amazing Mediterranean café at your expense. Then you took me shopping at multiple boutiques, all while giving a very in-depth tour of the town." I grab his hand and give it a small squeeze, "Seeing you again was the best thing that's happened to me since starting my vacation. I don't want to just be your guest; I want to help out and maybe even invest. My lawyer advised me to find something to invest in one day anyway. I would much rather invest in a person than just a business. Plus, I'm here to figure out my interests and passions, remember? Sounds like a lot of different projects I can research and maybe even observe." *Granted Alex has no education in accounting, she just mentioned I should look into it.* He looks over at me as we come to a stop at the red light. "From what I recall, you never were one to just sit by and watch when it came to passion." He gives my hand a small squeeze as I feel the blush spread across my face.

I shiver, "It looks like this storm caught the whole town off guard, it's no surprise that the deliveries have been delayed." I mention in a not-so-subtle attempt to change the topic. He adds that they should have had more generators in place, regardless of the delivery delays. "The mountains make crazy weather, but this was something else. Logan swears he's had a string of bad luck these past few months" he says while turning into a furniture store parking lot. "Hopefully Hawk has everything in stock and can have someone deliver everything before the storm. They're usually pretty quick." He adds while pulling to a stop and turning off the truck.

We unbuckle as he says, "I've got a budget and a list, what could go wr-" I immediately lean over and put my hand over his mouth, silencing him before he can effectively jinx us further. "You literally just said there has been bad luck lately and now you want to risk *more* bad luck?" I ask while looking into his steel gray eyes. *They're darker than they were earlier.* His nostrils flare as I slowly pull my hand back, trying not to notice how soft his lips feel. I look down at his lips. *I wonder if he's still a good kisser.* "Want to help pick out some beds, dressers, desks, and pretty much everything else needed to set up a few rooms?" he asks after a moment. *That's not what you wanted to ask me, but I'll let it go.* "That sounds fun" I agree as we climb out of the truck and head towards the entrance of the store

Thirty minutes later

Kris thanked Mr. Hawk as he handed the form back to the older gentleman. "I'll have Pecos deliver what we have in stock in about an hour. I can put an order in for the rest once I know what's on the incoming truck. It's a shame you're going to miss it, got some interesting pieces coming. Hopefully we can have everything delivered by the end of next week, depending on this weather." Mr. Hawk says with a thick accent that I can't place. "Do you know when the snow is supposed to fall?" Kris asks as I excuse myself to go find the restroom. "It's been delayed until late tonight, last I heard." Mr. Hawke turns towards me. "I believe the plumber is still fixing the one in the main building, and I wouldn't recommend the one in the workshop." He nods towards the back. "Why don't you head next door and use the guest bathroom at the house? I can assure you it's cleaned more often" Mr. Hawk adds with a chuckle. Kris smiles and nods, "I can confirm Mr. Hawke keeps his place very clean and he expects guests to leave it clean." He adds as though he learned from experience. "I can show you where it is." I nod and follow him outside. "Tsaaku mia" Mr. Hawke says with a wave.

"You two seem close, also what did he say while we were leaving?" I say with a smile as we walk towards a three-story cabin behind the furniture store. "Tsaaku mia, it's the Numunuu phrase for 'go in a good way'. Mr. Hawk taught me how to make things with my hands, and then he taught me how to take care of

72

those things. I would work here part time just to get more time to learn from him" Kris smiles as we walk up to a beautiful log cabin. "Mr. Hawke's wife passed a long time ago, so it's been just him and his son for the past 20 years. They built this in honor of her. She and Mr. Hawke always wanted a big multigenerational house to be passed down, filled with love and laughter." Kris stops on the porch as a big delivery truck pulls into the furniture store parking lot. "It's beautiful, did they carve this?" I ask while gently touching the animals carved into the wood. "Yes, they did, it took them years to finish everything inside." He replies and I pause to look over at the delivery truck.

"I believe that's the truck they were waiting on. We may get everything we need today after all. I'll show you where the bathroom is" Kris replies while opening the painted door. I stop and point over my shoulder, "Why don't you go see whatever it was that Mr. Hawke wanted to show you? I can meet you at the truck when I'm done" I say, knowing he's dying to see what's on the truck. He looks at me and frowns, "You are still my guest. I can't just leave you at a friend's house to go shopping" I scoff and reply "Kris I'm a big girl; I can go to the bathroom by myself. Go look at furniture, shoo shoo." I say while pushing him gently towards the stairs. He laughs "Alright. If I don't see you at the truck in 10 minutes, I'll head back here. The bathroom is down the hallway in front of you as you walk in the door. Second door on your left." He waits for me to open the door before he starts walking towards the delivery truck. Mr. Hawke waves at him excitedly and I laugh.

I walk inside the cabin and take in the beautiful carvings and furniture. Each piece holding painstakingly detailed carvings. *I've never seen such beautiful craftsmanship.* I walk down the hall and open the second door on my left, noticing a very detailed bronze statue in the corner. *They wrapped a towel around him for modesty, how cute. I wonder if I can find something I enjoy doing in this town. The people are so kind, plus I already know one person here.* After I finish my business and wash my hands, I notice even the sink looks like it was carved locally from the mountain stone. *A few hours ago, you couldn't leave this place fast enough. Now that an old lover has appeared, are you're thinking about staying permanently?* My wise inner me asks and I shake my head. "You are thirty and thriving, no need to stay in one place, Sabrina. You can find your passion anywhere in the world" I snicker as I open the bathroom door and walk right into the bronze statue. *Or here. I really like it here.*

I gasp and brace my hands against the statue, instantly feeling warm skin. My eyes are glued to the water droplets slowly trailing down his perfectly sculpted chest. I watch in frozen horror as my hand moves over the smooth bronzed skin, as though he were indeed a statue placed here for me to explore. I touch the water droplet and hear a sharp inhale; I yank my hand away while stepping back. "I am so sorry. Mr. Hawk said I could use the bathroom here and I didn't think anyone else was here. I didn't mean to touch you; I thought you were a statue." I close my mouth before I can continue rambling as the bronze statue laughs and crosses his arms. "I'm Pecos, his son. And you are?" he adds after a moment. "Oh, I'm sorry, my name is Sabrina, Sabrina Eldwin." *Why do I always touch first and introduce myself second?* He looks at my outstretched hand with a smile. "I suppose we haven't touched enough for one day" He says with a wink before grasping my hand in an easy shake. I feel my face getting hotter by the second as his brown eyes look into mine.

The door opens and Kris walks in with a grin, "Hey Pecos, I see you've met Ms. Eldwin. She's staying at the Retreat for the next month. She's also helping me pick some new furniture while we are in town. You think you can beat the storm this evening? If not, bring a bag and bunk with me and Logan tonight. It can be just like old times" he asks as Pecos looks back to me. "Absolutely, but your guest might try to steal my innocence, will you offer protection?" He asks seriously as I cough and blush. Kris laughs as Pecos winks at me again and I blush harder. *Who winks that much?* "I'll wait for you by the truck" I say while walking away from a potentially mortifying conversation. I hear Pecos's deep laugh as Kris asks him what

74

happened. I sigh and walk faster to the truck, hearing Kris's laughter in the background.

CHAPTER FIFTEEN

~Logan~

November 14th
4:10pm

As I step onto the porch from the kitchen, Kristian pulls in with a full truck load. *The dark clouds are still far off, but that can change quick up here. I'm glad I finished the floors in the guest room early.* As I walk closer, I see Sabrina's silhouette in the passenger seat and freeze. *What do I say to her?* As I think on how best to approach her, she looks up and sees me. She opens the door and immediately apologizes, "I am so sorry for knocking you out earlier". She takes her shades off and looks at me with the most crystal blue eyes I have ever seen. *Whoa.* I stare at the woman in front of me. Her shiny black hair hangs loose in soft waves, stopping just above her shoulders. *Is this the same woman? Her eyes are blue now, really blue.* She smiles at me and I feel my shoulders relax. *Yep, same woman.*

I smile and hold out my hands towards Kristian. "It's alright. I scared you and you reacted the same way my mom does." Kristian comes around holding a box, grinning like a fool. "Wait till you hear what she did to poor Pecos. Be careful Logan, Bri's a man eater" he adds while laughing. "Kris!" she says while blushing. I narrow my eyes at Kristian in a subtle attempt to remind him that she is a guest. "It looks like you both are getting along well. By the way, do your eyes shift from green to blue?" I ask while staring at her eyes. "I've worn green contacts for the past few years. This morning, I decided it was time to throw them away. My eyes would draw unwanted attention at work." she adds while grabbing her bag, beating Kristian to it. "Bri and are old friends that lost touch about 10 years ago. Neither of us recognized each other until we got our hair cut" Kris says while looking at her fondly.

That explains their behavior. "Mr. Logan, we found another loose board up here" I turned my head to see Luna leaning from a window upstairs, waving at me. *Probably shouldn't say that in front of guests.* I chuckle and wave back to her, telling her I will be right there. "Ms. Eldwin, did Kristian explain the arrangements for tonight?" I ask, hoping he talked to her already. "Why are you calling me Ms. Eldwin now? You weren't calling me that last night" she says while gathering the rest of her things from the back. Kristian snorts as I pick up her suitcase and bag, both much heavier than I recall. "I was trying to be polite since you are our guest" I reply as she turns towards me. "You knew I was your guest last night too. Kris told me what you said, I believe you said I looked like a 'cute gray mouse' when you were rescuing me. This was before he gave me a wonderful tour of Boulder Springs, 10 stars by the way." she replies with a mischievous glint in her eye. *Point one to Sabrina.*

Kristian coughs and she smiles, "I'm an open book boys, don't tell me a secret." I laugh and start bringing her things inside. "Well then, Sabrina, I hope you had a great time. Do you have any places you want to revisit? You reserved multiple tours of the town and area so I'm sure we will be able to revisit some." She goes on to tell me about the tour and her favorite parts of the town as we set her bags in her room. She grins, "I want to eat at a few more places over there. I saw a bakery where everything was made in clay stoves." I nod to her. "I think I know which place you're talking about. They offer classes there on the weekends." I add as we walk back to the truck. Kristian passes us with more boxes, "I believe Logan saved a few muffins from Mr. Jenkins earlier" he says as Sabrina immediately turns towards the kitchen. I laugh and tell her they are in the basket on the counter as I walk outside to finish unloading the truck.

Later

After we finish unloading the truck, I follow Kristian inside and hand Sabrina her room keys. "Do you want me to start preparing for dinner?" Willow asks and I groan. *It's after 4pm already?* "Yes, but don't put anything in the oven until 5pm. Do you remember where the meal plan book is?" She holds up a brown worn book and nods. "Ah you already have it, good. I need to head upstairs to fix the floorboard." I say as she starts to pull vegetables from the refrigerator. "Luna already fixed the floorboard; she is working on the dresser now. We took off the broken closet door and blocked the deck entrance with it for now." She replies casually. I narrow my eyes. *She fixed the floor and is now working on the dresser?* "I'll go up and thank her, as well as inspect for safety. We should have furniture delivered soon, so it's going to be busy around here. I'll need someone keeping the floors dry so we don't slip." I say as Kristian walks towards the front door. "We should go ahead and do final checks before the storm rolls in" he adds as Willow nods to us. "We will have everything ready. Luna says from the stairs. *When did she get there?* I close the door behind me and grin. *This might work out after all.* I start making the rounds, not noticing there was a little more pep in my step.

45 minutes later

"So, you met in college, had a few hot encounters, and then never spoke to each other again? That's it?" I say after closing the last cabinet in the Woodline cabin. "I mean, it doesn't sound like much when you put it like that, and it wasn't just a few. It was most of summer after my last year of college." Kristian says as he opens the refrigerator. "Remember when I stayed in Florida for that internship after college? I met her at a festival of sorts, and we spent the rest of the summer together. We ended things pretty well too. There was no arguing or anything like that. We agreed it would be better to preserve the memory of a perfect summer, than to try and force something that wouldn't last long term." His shoulders drop a little and I frown before asking, "Sounds like you still have feelings for her. Will you be okay here with her?" He chuckles and inspects the drawer as he replies, "She was my best friend. We weren't exclusive or anything, she

78

didn't even tell me her real last name. Even after ten years, we both slipped right back into familiarity as soon as we ran into each other. Well, the second time, when we recognized each other, I mean." I laugh as he shuts the drawer and stands.

Kristian looks at me before adding, "I was trying to explain that she doesn't want a refund nor is she holding us to a high standard, no offense." I chuckle as he closes the empty refrigerator. "Believe it or not, I actually have high hopes for this weekend. I want to show off my culinary skills for a change." I say as I walk towards the door. Kristian grins, "She signed up for everything you offered on the website. I still don't know how you are going to fit everything in the schedule with just the two of us to lead hikes and tours, plus maintenance." I nod and rub my beard. "I didn't expect someone to pick everything we offered during one stay. Thankfully we have a month to work everything in" I add as he picks up the tool bag and follows me towards the door. "She came here to learn something and is looking for somewhere to start fresh. She wants to take every class so she can see what she likes." I hold the door open for him as he continues, "What if she likes cooking and wants to stay as your new cook? Or maybe she falls in love with hiking and wants to be a guide?" I stop on the porch and grab his arm before he continues. "Kristian, do you want her to stay? You see her for the first time in over a decade, and you are already planning for her to drop everything and stay?" I ask, the shock evident in my voice.

He shakes my hand off and scowls at me. "No man, it isn't like that." He puts his hands on the rails and says, "She would be good for this place, I can feel it." He looks at me with sincerity before adding, "She would be good for you too, she has a way with people." I smirk at his words "Well, I support you, but don't get us sued." He laughs and heads towards the B&B "She called you a sexy man-bear by the way, how about *you* don't get us sued." He added as I slip on a patch of ice. "You're making that up!" I yell at his retreating form. *What is that anyway?* I start to imagine man-bear creatures and shake my head at the impression I must have given her. *She must think I'm a brute or something.*

Catching up to Kristian, I see the Hawk's delivery truck pull to a stop in front of the B&B. "Hey Pecos, great timing. Looks like it may storm early so let's get unloaded. We can sort out where to put everything later tonight." Kristian says while opening Pecos's door. "You're about as patient as Sabrina" Pecos says after stepping down, smiling back at Kristian. "Am I the only one that is still treating her like a guest that paid a lot of money to be here?" I scowl at them for speaking so casually. "Well maybe because on the way over here, I told Kris I was thinking of investing in this place." I look to my right and see Sabrina standing with her hands on her hips smirking at me. "I trust my instincts. This sounds like a fun adventure and who knows, this place could be a new source of happiness for me. It's the perfect time to do something like this. Also, I've seen everyone here shirtless, we are at least all friends at this point, right?" She says nonchalantly. Kristian laughs as I furrow my brows. *I can't figure her out.*

"I thought you were looking for passions all over the world, are you sure you want to settle for a few locals in the first town you visit?" Pecos says with a smirk while walking towards her. *I can imagine the smoldering look he is giving her right now, has everyone lost their mind?* Sabrina blushes, "I was talking about hobbies, not people. And to be fair, I thought you were a statue." Kris chuckles after rolling out the ramp on the truck. "Maybe you should look for a sculpting class, then you can make your own-" Kristian coughs, interrupting Pecos before saying, "Pecos, stop teasing Sabrina. They call him the Pahayoko around here, don't take anything he says seriously" He looks at Sabrina who nods in return. "Let's get this unloaded so Pecos can be back before the storm hits" I say while looking at the ominous clouds rolling in. Pecos nods and mentions he has some things he needs to take care of after finishing up here. He freezes and his head snaps towards the B&B. Kristian and I follow his gaze, knowing his instincts are never wrong.

Luna walks awkwardly in the snow, her arms fidgeting as

80

she continues towards us. I look back at Pecos and notice his stiff frame and narrowed eyes. *Maybe I should look into their background more.* Glancing at Kristian I can tell he is thinking the same thing. Pecos watches as I step down to see what Luna needs. "Is everything okay?" I ask as she looks nervously around. "Oh yes, everything is wonderful and working properly. Willow wanted to know if we should prepare for an extra guest. She also wanted to know what time to have dinner ready" she looks towards Pecos and rubs her hands together. A white lifted truck pulls in and Mr. Hawk waves to us from the cab. "Yes, prepare for a few extra guests. Go ahead and have extra bedding ready in case the Hawkes stay the night as well. They will be in Kristian and I's room with Pecos. 6:30pm or 7pm will work for dinner. If she needs anything or has any questions, come get me." I say as Sabrina and Kristian walk over to greet Mr. Hawk. Luna nods and turns back towards the B&B.

"What was that about?" I ask Pecos once Luna reaches the porch. "Nothing, why is my father here?" He replies curtly. "I'm not sure. Kristian went to check, but it looks like they are headed over here. Did you get a bad feeling about Lunabella?" His eyes soften, "Lunabella? So that's her name" he looks back at the B&B with an unreadable expression on his face. "I hired her and her sister today, do I need to dig into their past?" His nostrils flare as his eyes snap to mine. "That isn't necessary. I don't think she is a threat" he adds. *Oh.* I grin, realizing he was attracted to her. "Listen Pahayoko, she isn't available." He looks at me and narrows his eyes, "She's married?" I shake my head. "Worse, an overprotective older sister." I laugh at the scowl now covering his face. *Oh yes, your worst nightmare, protective family.*

Glancing over to my left, I see his father approaching. Sabrina and Kristian follow beside him before turning to walk up the ramp of the truck. Mr. Hawk greets me and turns to his son, "Pecos, I need the delivery truck to move the donated beds to the shelter before the storm. We can unload everything into the yard here, and then you four can move it wherever it needs to go. You can drive my truck back to the house tomorrow if it gets too late." Mr. Hawk looks up to the sky and then at Pecos before adding something low. "Let's get to work then" Kristian says while slapping my back.

CHAPTER SIXTEEN

~Sabrina~

6pm

I lean against the edge of an armchair as Pecos and Logan bring in the last bit of furniture. "Can you set the desk in front of the window over there instead?" I ask as I point to the large window near the deck entrance. "That's much better." I say after they set it down. Logan grins at me, "I appreciate this Sabrina. I know nothing about how to make a room 'flow' as you put it" He adds as Luna walks up to the open doorway. "Mr. Logan, Willow is ready for you in the kitchen." She says, her pale green eyes glancing at the furniture. Logan nods and heads downstairs. Luna turns to follow him as Pecos narrows his eyes at her retreating back. I put my hands on my hips after she is out of hearing distance, "Okay what's going on with you two?" She hasn't looked at you once and yet, you can't stop looking at her. To be honest, I can't tell if you are staring or glaring. It's getting kind of creepy." I say firmly and he frowns.

He stays silent for a moment. "I didn't mean to be creepy." He says while rubbing the bridge between his nose. "I want to talk to her, but I can't find the words once she is close. That's never happened before" he adds, looking like a lost puppy. "You like her" I say while grinning. "I know nothing about her. I only know her name from hearing Logan mention it." He scoffs and walks towards me, leaning down he softly adds, "Does this mean you are no longer interested in exploring my body? Or, perhaps you enjoy sharing?" He smirks and I feel my face heat up. I match his gaze and see the mischief in his eyes. I reply, "Nice deflection. Yes, I did get distracted by your muscles, but come on! Who wouldn't? That isn't fair, even Kris admitted to sneaking a pe-"

I clamp my mouth shut and avert my eyes while he laughs. *Kris is going to fuss at me for sure.* "You didn't answer the part about sharing" he says with a grin. I lean in, "Sharing is caring, right? If everyone involved is fine with it, of course." I reply after licking my lips. He smirks and I realize how close we are.

I jump as Luna says, "If you two would like to use this room tonight, we can swap." Pecos moves so fast, there is a small breeze between us as he steps away from me. *Anytime now Earth.* As I wait to be absorbed by mother nature, Pecos looks at Luna. "No. This room is perfect for you. Kris and I already agreed to fix the railing for the deck tomorrow." He says softly, his eyes never leaving her. *Oh my. He really does have a crush on Luna!* I squeal inside as I get to watch their moment. "I went out there earlier, it looked beautiful. Did you know Orion is supposed to be visible to the naked eye starting tonight? I hope the storm goes by quickly so we can see it" she wiggles a little as her hands fidget in excitement. Pecos smiles and I swear I feel my heart skip a beat for her. "You shouldn't go out there until we fix the railing, little deer, it would be dangerous. You wouldn't want to worry anyone, would you?" He asks while crossing his arms, still smiling at her. Luna's eyes dart around "Oh, I wouldn't want to be a bother, no, no." She starts to rub her hands together and Pecos frowns. "You aren't a bother" he says gently. She shakes her head "I won't go out there. I should go see if anyone needs anything." She turns and heads back down the stairs before either of us can get a word in.

I look at Pecos as he curses, "See? Now she thinks she's a bother. I don't even know how that happened" He runs his hand through his long black hair and sighs. "That's because she has something unresolved. Didn't you hear her say she didn't want to be a bother *again*? That implied someone had told her she was a bother before." I pause while he contemplates my words. "I think she might have wanted to avoid that feeling, so she decided to avoid putting herself in a similar situation." I pat his arm as his frown deepens "I'll see you at dinner. I hope you brought an overnight bag, Kris won't let you leave now that the snow is falling this much" I turn and head down the stairs to see Willow working in the kitchen and Luna setting the table. I wave to them as I enter the kitchen. Pecos passes me and walks to the front door, grabbing his coat along the way. "Just getting my bag from the truck. I'll be back in a moment." He says towards Luna, closing the door behind him firmly. I turn and see Luna rubbing her hands again.

One hour later

I lean back in the chair and pat my full belly. "That was amazing, thank you" I say to Willow and Logan. "Don't thank me, I barely did anything" Logan says while smiling at Willow. "That's not true Mr. Logan; you seasoned everything and wrote the recipe for my sister to follow. Since she made no alterations to your recipe, it wouldn't have tasted like this without your joint efforts" Luna says while gathering the dirty dishes. Kris grins after wiping his mouth. "Who wants pecan pie? I made 3 different types; Salted caramel, chocolate, and maple." Willow asks while standing up. "Yes" I say immediately. Logan chuckles as he stands "Pecos might want some. He ate pretty quickly and then went upstairs. Luna, would you mind asking him which one he wants? We also have ice cream if he prefers that" Logan adds while starting the line for pie. Luna nods and sets the dirty dishes in the sink before heading towards the stairs.

I stand behind Logan while Kris contemplates which pie he wants to try first. Willow smiles while setting them out. "I hope you like them" she says after handing us our dessert plates. "I think the issue is, do we have enough? Bri said she was full, now she's contemplating how many slices she will stash for midnight snacks. Did you know that at 19, she won a pizza eating contest. She didn't even bat an eyelash when they rolled out desert afterwards, just started grabbing sweets. That's when she stole my heart." Kris laughs and I make a heart symbol with my hands. "I do enjoy food" I stick my tongue out as Logan stares at us. As Willow steps into the pantry to reorganize the shelves, I excuse myself to go to the bathroom. After I turn the corner, I pause to pick up the back of my earring and I hear the conversation pick up again.

"I don't know how to do this" Logan says with a huff. "What do you mean?" Kris asks Logan as they walk back to the table with their pie. "How are we supposed to take Sabrina's money after she helped us unload a delivery truck. She is our guest; you shouldn't ask guests to unload delivery trucks, Kristian." Logan says with a grimace. "Technically, she paid in advance so we already took her money and *then* we had her help unload a delivery truck." I frown as Kristian jokes about the situation. "She was serious about wanting to invest. She had some good ideas too. Look what she has done already with organizing the furniture, it looks way better than us just tossing it where it fits, don't you think?" He asks casually. "So you want to hire her? Do you know how hard I worked to stay professional about this whole thing? I had everything planned out and scheduled, now everyone is planning slumber parties while blizzards wreck the schedule." I hear a fork get set down and Kris replies, softer this time. "You kept saying everything was fine, this internal struggle of yours isn't 'fine'. Burying your issues isn't the answer. Sabrina is the best first guest we could ask for. If these issues happened with anyone else, we probably would have been sued. Oh, and she doesn't care about the weather messing up plans, *trust me*." I feel my face flushing as memories from college invade my mind once again. *Should I still be eavesdropping?*

"What if someone takes a joke too far? What if she doesn't get everything she paid for, and changes her mind? It's been a *decade* Kristian. Can you really say without a doubt, that she hasn't changed?" Logan asks with an edge to his voice. *I don't blame him at all. Alex would love the manbear.* I grab the pen and legal pad on the entryway table as I take a deep breath. "I can answer that. In fact, I can sign a sworn statement of intent right now" I smile as I poke my head around the corner. "Yes, I eavesdropped. It was rude and I apologize. Now let's work this out" I sit down at the table and place the legal pad and pen next me. I pick up my fork for a quick bite as they collect themselves. "I thought you had to use the bathroom?" Kris says narrowing his eyes at me. I slowly chew my pie, doing my best to keep my composure as the chocolate melts in my mouth. "Only to make sure I didn't have food my teeth. I used the hall mirror around the corner instead, Also, this is the best chocolate pecan pie I have ever had." Kris laughs as I fork another bite into my mouth and moan. "I am so glad you like it, here you go" Willow hands me a glass of water. I nod to her in thanks as Luna walks around the corner. Snow falls from her hair as she fidgets, "I need pie" she says with a determined look on her face.

CHAPTER SEVENTEEN

~Pecos~

Earlier

I blink my eyes as more snow flurries impede my vision. *I'll have about 5 minutes before I won't be able to see well enough to work. I should be able to finish in time if I buckle down.* I grab another spindle and continue to work on the railing. So lost in my thoughts; I don't hear the balcony door open behind me. *What was Logan thinking by putting her in this room? I will need to check the rest of the building tomorrow. What if she trips over a broken board out here and falls through the railing?* I narrow my eyes and continue thinking about a certain blonde that walks like a fawn. Blinking out the snow gathering in my eyes, I continue working, getting further drawn into my own musings.

After making my way to the end of the balcony, I can barely see where the last top rail fits. Light shines on the hole and I look up to see Lunabella wrapped in a quilt. She holds the lantern near the railing, her hair blowing in the wind. "Little deer why are you here?" I ask, unable to keep the surprise out of my voice. "We can talk later. You wanted to finish before the storm, right?" She replied while looking at the railing. "It's too cold out here, go back downstairs" I say gently. She shakes her head, and moves the lantern closer to me instead. "I have a few more things to work on once I finish out here. I don't have time to entertain you right now." I hear the edge in my voice and instantly wish I could retract my words. "I see. I apologize." She replies and sets the lantern down, angling it so it still shines where I need it. "That's not I meant, wait-" I say as she closes the door softly behind her. I blow out a sigh of frustration. *I didn't mean it like that.* I frown and continue working.

~Sabrina~

After announcing her need for pie, we watch in silence as Luna takes a slice of each pie and puts them on small plates, her mouth drawn in a tight line. "Luna, is everything okay?" Willow asks as Luna huffs before grabbing a tray. "Pecos barely ate anything. He's working on the railing because he thinks it's a safety hazard that we or more specifically, I am unable to avoid. He was there when Mr. Kristian made us sign waivers and specifically told us not to go out there anymore, why is he being so stubborn?" She looks at Logan. He groans and rubs his face. "I told him we would work on the railings tomorrow. Why would he think you would wander out there despite all the warnings? We even agreed to put a lock on the balcony door in case either of you sleepwalk" he sighs again as Willow gathers the leftover dishes.

Kris looks towards the sisters and says "Why don't we take the pie up to Pecos, while you and your sister clean up? I also need one of you to ensure the bathrooms are fully stocked" Luna nods and walks to the stove while rolling up her sleeves as Willow heads towards the pantry. *Neither of them said a word, yet they already knew which tasks to do. That's handy.* "What can I do to help?" I ask while looking at Logan. I pull my hair back into a short ponytail as he scowls at me. "Does it even matter what I say? Did you seriously pay to come here and move furniture? Is that what thrills you?" I look at him and smile mischievously before leaning towards him, "Would you believe me if I said this was the most fun that I've had in ten years?" I lean closer and whisper, "And just how would you thrill me, Mr. Hale?" Willow coughs to cover her laugh as she walks towards the living room with a basket full of toiletries. I lean back as Logan scowls, throwing his arms up in defeat. "Don't forget we need to sit down and write a letter of intent later" I wink at him as he follows Kristian upstairs.

Willow motions for me to join her in the living room. "Would you mind taking a peek at your room and let me know what you think? I also restocked the bathroom for you with the new soaks that came in" I thank her and walk into my room, gasping as I open the door. *The new jade rug accents the hardwood floors perfectly.* I walk towards the light purple chair facing the small corner fireplace. Biting my lip, I sink into the soft, yet supportive cushion. *This is amazing, I need one for my future place.* I make a mental note to have Mr. Hawk furnish my future home. I look at the empty picture frames scattered along the walls, waiting to be filled with art. *I wonder if he will use local artists.* The fire crackles softly in the background, lulling me to sleep. I don't notice as someone drapes a blanket over me.

~Pecos~

"I still don't see why both of you brought me pie. 3 slices of pie to be exact." I grumble as I take off my boots. "I still don't see why you couldn't wait until tomorrow to fix the railing like we agreed on" Logan replies sarcastically. "Luna prepared this for you. We wanted to bring it and see if maybe we could help, since it's our responsibility. Kris adds with a smile. "You act as though we're not all brothers by choice. We have shared many things over the years, don't make it weird over a railing." I reply while grabbing a plate of pie. "That one is chocolate I believe" Logan says after sitting in a white wooden chair. I take a bite and walk around the white divider screen to get the other chair. *It's good.* I remind myself to thank Willow later.

After sitting down in the chair, I continue eating as Kris grabs a slice of pie on the way to the corner of the room. "We should build a closet tomorrow if there isn't damage from the storm. The 'L' shape of the room makes it difficult to use dressers." Logan pauses to think as Kris opens the white wardrobe to remove the sealing tape. "It's perfect for a walk-through closet. Willow said they have no problem sharing dressers since they don't have many clothes" Kris adds before closing the mirrored wardrobe facing Willow's side of the room. *Why don't they have more clothes? That isn't your business, focus.* I shake my head, "If there's nothing going on at the store then I can help" I add before spooning another heaping helping of pie into my mouth. "I'll want a pie weekly as payment" I add.

Logan huffs, "Watch out Pecos, Kristian already lured Ms. Eldwin into becoming an investor, you could be next." I smirk, "I have no money to invest". Kris chuckles as he walks towards Logan, "Just so you know, I tried to talk her out of investing. Don't act like you aren't thrilled at the way things have turned out. I know I'm not the only one here drawn to her. Logan, weren't you venting this morning about how wrong your attraction to her was because she was a guest?" He turns towards me, "Say something Pecos, she all but drooled on you earlier and you loved the attention too". Logan looks at me and grins. "That was before he saw the moon in broad daylight." He adds as Kris's laughter fills the room. I shake my head as Logan start to chuckle and makes more jokes.

After their laughter dies down, Logan sets down his empty plate and I frown. "You came to help fix the railing, yet you *watched* me finish it instead of doing anything. You ate the pie intended for me and now tell me I may have to share *another* female with you? Nope, I'm out. Good luck to you both." I stand and put everything back on the tray. "Looks like it's down to you and me now" Kris says with a laugh, throwing his arm around Logan's shoulders. "Let's go see what else need to get done tonight" I add as they continue to bicker behind me. "So does this mean you want to invest?" Kris wiggles his eyebrows at me, and I can't help but laugh. "I have a lot of free time now that the renovations for my brother and his fiancé are done. I can invest my time and talents, but that's about it." Krist slaps his other arm around my shoulder and tells me that's more than he could have asked for. Logan shimmies out from under Kris's arm and shakes his head. He opens the door and we start down the stairs.

Five Hours Later

Logan

I wake up to a chill in the air and frown. *The power must be out again.* I move to add a log to the fireplace and look around the living room for the lantern. *Willow assured me her and Luna would take care of their fireplace.* Once I finish in the living room, I walk down the hall and I open the door to my room. Waves of snores assault me as I chuckle. *I wonder if the paintings can fall off the walls from their vibrations.* Pecos and Kristian alternate between harmonizing and gutturals in their snore-off as I throw a few logs in the fireplace. After closing the door behind me, I notice there is no glow under Sabrina's door. I frown and walk down the hall, softly knocking on her door once I reach it.

Once I feel an appropriate amount of time has passed, I knock again. "Sabrina? It's Logan, do you need any firewood?" I wait for an answer before adding "I'm going to come in and check the fireplace, okay?" I pause, debating on morals and ethics vs warmth and safety. I knock a little louder, and wait for an acknowledgement. *Keep your eyes on the floor and straight to the fireplace.* I open the door to a dark room. The red coals from the fireplace glare at me as I quickly walk over to put a log on them. I stir them around until they catch flame again. A soft snore alerts me, and I look to my right to see Sabrina shivering in the chair.

That blanket isn't nearly enough to warm her with the fire out. I frown before whispering "Sabrina, wake up you need to move to the bed." I shake her arm lightly. "Sabrina, I need you to go to bed." I say a little louder. She huffs, "I swear daddy, you are so bossy" She grabs the blanket as she stands before trudging to the bed, keeping her eyes closed. I quickly rush over to move the covers, so she doesn't lay on top of them. She plops down and starts to snore softly. I clamp my mouth shut as I drape the covers over her. I start walking back to the living room, shoulders shaking with suppressed laughter. Only after I reach the couch do I let it out. I shake out the blanket and drape it over myself before drifting off to sleep. The sound of my snores join the symphony at the Retreat.

CHAPTER EIGHTEEN

~Sabrina~

November 15th
8am

I wake up to the pleasant smell of coffee, and something I can't quite put my finger on. *It smells delicious, whatever it is.* I swing my legs around the edge of the bed to start my morning stretches. *I need to go for a run later if they keep adding pie to the menu.* Afterwards, I walk over to my suitcase, still unpacked by the new dresser. While grabbing some clothes, I hear laughter outside and smile. I peek through the curtain to see Luna and Pecos engaged in a fierce snowball fight. *They look cute together.* I make a mental note to see if my skills as a matchmaker will be needed later as I walk into the bathroom. The sunlight pours in from the window, and I find myself staring at the smeared make-up on my face. I stare back at the racoon eyed woman. *So glad no one saw me like this, they would have been terrified.* I giggle and turn on the light, "The power is on too? It's going to be a fantastic day" I close the window curtain, strip, and step into the warm spray. *Finally time to start my vacation, for real this time.* I sigh and relax as the water flows over me.

After showering, I check my phone to see if Alex replied to the torrent of pictures I sent yesterday. *No notifications, but it's only 10:30am down there. She was probably working on that big case all day yesterday. Hopefully, they celebrated a big win, and she got to sleep in.* Lost in thought, I open the door and walk right into Logan. He reaches out to steady me as I brace my palms against his chest. "Easy there. You alright?" He asks with concern, his brown eyes gazing into mine. "Yes, sorry I was thinking about something and wasn't paying attention." I inhale his marshmallow scent, still confused on why he always smells like my favorite snack. *Pull yourself together, Sabrina!* "Is that coffee I smell?" I move around him before my treacherous hands start exploring him like Isle De Pecos yesterday. He laughs and follows me towards the kitchen. *He knows.*

"Why yes, it is. Is your goal to fondle everyone here? Willow you may want to set some boundaries with Sabrina before she sets her eyes on you next." Kris says with his blue eyes twinkling with mischief. *Curse my wandering hands!* My face flushes as Willow laughs, "Maybe I would like the attention, you never know." She smiles at me while pouring a cup of coffee. Kris laughs as Logan scowls at him. "Need I remind you, she is still a guest that paid to be here." I poke Logan's arm lightly and reply on Kris's behalf, "Need I remind *you* I signed a legal pad last night stating that I was no longer staying as just a guest, but as a friend and potential investor. That means no more overuse of manners, or it'll feel like you just want me for my money." I smile and walk into the kitchen as he scowls. Willow hands me a pretty purple mug with gray mountains on it and points to the bar set up with a tea and coffee dressing station.

"Thank you so much" I say as she pours another cup. Logan leans towards me and whispers, "You know that isn't true." I nod to him, smiling as I add a heavy pour of chocolate sauce. I grab a spoon from the drawer and turn towards Kris. "Did the storm fizzle out or are they normally that short?" I ask while stirring. "It varies, but the weather here lately has been odd. The power was only out for a few hours last night, and there was no damage that we found. We already shoveled the paths and cleaned up around the property. All in all, I'd say we were lucky. We already figured the hike would need to be rescheduled so you and Logan can work on the schedule later." Kris replied and grabs his cup of coffee. "I booked everything available on the website, and I truly have no schedule of my own. I'm fine with whatever, whenever." I add before sipping my coffee.

"I bet you are" Pecos says from behind me. I spit my coffee

out as Kris roars with laughter and hands me a towel. "That's it, Pecos. I'm getting you a bell" I say with a laugh. Luna looks down and starts tapping her fingers together. She smiles and excuses herself to start laundry. She takes the coffee-stained towel and walks up the stairs. Willow turns towards me and says, "Please let me know what you would like for breakfast, and I will fix you a plate" She lifts the lids off of the warmers and I point to the jalapeño maple grain links and a few other options. "Pecos, would you like anything else?" She asks him with an odd expression. "Yes, thank you" He replies while grabbing a slice of chocolate pecan pie.

I eyeball his pie and remember that I am a grown woman on vacation, pie is an option for breakfast. *Yes, but you just spent a ridiculous amount for one dress in many colors, you shouldn't risk gaining wei-* My thoughts are interrupted as a slice of caramel pecan pie is placed in front of me. White cool whip flowers drizzled in chocolate sauce are spread around the plate. I look up and Logan smiles back at me before grabbing a biscuit. *I like you.* Never one to turn down a chance to try new things, I pick up the fork. My eyes close as I take a bite of the pie. I am instantly transported out of my body into a spiral of decadence. *What kind of magic caramel is this?* I take another bite with some of the whipped cream this time. Unable to escape the sounds coming from my body, I melt into the flavors my taste buds are experiencing. *It's homemade.* I take another bite and moan. *I don't know how much time has passed, and I don't care. I'm in love. I want this every day, for the rest of my life.*

My eyes snap open as a cough interrupts my foodgasm-induced marriage to my pie. Willow turns around, shoulders shaking from suppressed laughter as Pecos does the same. Two more pie plates appear in front of me as I turn to see Kris and Logan grinning down at me. I blush and smack Kris's arm as he says, "I forgot you *really* like food. I see why breakfast can be a great start to someone's day". Everyone laughs and I put my hands on my hips with a smirk. "Jokes on who? I get more pie and you both get more action in a few minutes than either of you have in years. Seems like a win/win to me" I reply with a wink as Logan and Kris share shocked expressions. Pecos bellows with laughter so infectious, we all start laughing.

Luna walks in as we compose ourselves. She smiles and nods to Willow, who then excuses herself. "Let's do another check of the cabins before we start working on the other railings" Kris says after putting his arm around Logan's shoulders. They walk to the kitchen door as Luna turns towards me and asks, "Would you like for me to take your laundry and tidy your room for you? If there is anything you are uncomfortable with me touching, doing, or saying, please make a list for me to study." Luna smiles while holding out her hands. "I appreciate what you said yesterday, about wanting to be friends. I don't want to be presumptuous though" she adds. I smile, remembering a similar conversation I had with Layla. "I'm an open book with no OCDs. I promise I will let you know if you cross a line, but you have to do the same" I hold up my pinky as she grins and slowly loops hers awkwardly around mine. "I promise. I'm going to go clean your room now." She drops her hand quickly and walks into my room. I turn and notice Pecos leaning against the wall, our eyes meet and I grin.

He looks away and I smirk. "You like her" I say while crinkling my nose. He scoffs and unfolds his arms to push against the wall. "You're confused" he replies while walking towards the kitchen door. "Mhmmm" I say sarcastically. "I don't even know her" he adds sternly before stepping outside. "That still wasn't a no!" I yell as he closes the door behind him. *I saw those gorgeous lips smirk. Oh yea, he likes her.* I mentally squeal at the thought of getting to watch a live romance bloom on my vacation. *They are so awkward and adorable. I should help them, but how?* My brows furrow as I start to form together a plan. *Maybe Kris can invite Pecos to the thing I reserved tonight. Then we can all share dinner afterwards.* I smile at my brilliant plan as I take a bite of Logan's pie. *I love this pie. I don't even care if someone walks in, I'm finishing this time.*

CHAPTER NINETEEN

~Kristian~

12pm

A big pick-up truck pulls in as Logan and I walk around the corner of the Workers Respite cabin. "Marúawe, Mr. Hawke. How's everything in town?" I ask as Logan walks over to shake his hand. "Fine, fine. Thankfully, it left quick as it came with minimal damage." He grabs a bag out of the back of his truck before saying, "I brought some things for Pecos, I'm mighty glad a room was available. They say it'll be a week before everything is repaired. I booked him through your assistant an hour ago." He adds after noticing our confused expressions. "Ah, here comes the lovely lady now." Mr. Hawke walks past us with a grin. We turn to see Sabrina waving at us, her wavy shoulder-length hair bouncing with her movements. They embrace and walk inside as Logan and I scramble to catch up. *Bri, what have you done now?*

"Oh good, you're both here. Kris, can you show Mr. Hawke to the Painter's Retreat cabin while I go over everything with Logan? Pecos is already there." Sabrina says as soon as we walk in. Logan chuckles and replies instead, "I think I would rather get some ideas for the other cabins from Mr. Hawke. Mind if I escort him instead? I already trust Ms. Eldwin handled everything correctly" He looks at me with a smirk. *Sabrina, what did you do? I vouched for you and now you are conducting a not-so-hostile takeover of the Retreat, why?* I groan internally and nod. Sabrina smiles as Luna walks in to let us know lunch will be ready in twenty minutes. "We hope you stay for lunch Mr. Hawke, my sister made plenty." she adds as she wiggles her fingers by her sides. "If it isn't any trouble I'd love to. Better than my leftover hanisahuuba back home" She nods and goes back to the kitchen to help her sister as Logan takes the bags from Mr. Hawke. "Right this way sir" he says while opening the kitchen door. Once they are on the porch outside, I turn to confront Sabrina.

Of course she isn't there anymore. I groan and rub a hand over my face, "Luna, do you know where Sabrina went?" I ask dejectedly. "I believe she went upstairs to make a list of what each room needs." She replies before walking back to the kitchen. I turn towards the stairs while forming questions in my mind. *Why did you let Pecos stay in a cabin that was already reserved? Are you mad at me? Is this payback? Did you think about me at all in the last decade?* Shocked at the direction my thoughts are headed, I pause to collect myself before going down the hall lined with doors.

Sabrina opens the faded yellow door to my right and asks if I have a tape measure on me. "I do but first we need to talk" I say with as stern a voice as I can muster towards her. She laughs and closes the door in my face. *What is happening?* My mouth drops in shock as I hear something being moved. She reopens the door with a smile, "Sorry about that, I had the chair blocking the door. I was moving things around so I can start comparing paint vs wallpaper" she says while looking around the room. After I walk in and close the door behind me, I turn towards her and say. "We will come back to that later. I need to know why Pecos is staying in the cabin reserved for Mr. Pierson. What about your cabin, why not put him there? You didn't even consult us beforehand. You said you wanted to invest, but this feels more like a takeover" I lean closer to her and she frowns, "Did you miss me at all?" I ask as her blue eyes shift to mine. *I can almost see the mischief swirling in her eyes.*

She walks to the window and looks towards the snow-covered trees, "Mr. Pierson called to reschedule his stay. It is now for November 23rd-December 7th. He gave me a list of requests for things to be ready in his room upon his arrival. Everything was paid for in advance via the link Logan sent him in the

98

original reservation. Copies of all documents are available for review on Logan's desk." She explains with a smirk. I ask why she didn't come get us and she narrows her eyes. "When Mr. Pierson called, Willow couldn't find you or Logan so of course I asked if I could take a message for the owners. When he explained he needed to reschedule or he would have to cancel, I had Logan's books open on the table in two-seconds flat and rescheduled him myself." I feel my face heat up with shame for jumping to conclusions. *Logan said she probably handled everything fine, I'm the one that overreacted this time.* I grimace, now understanding his smirk wasn't about her messing up, it was about *me* messing up.

Her eyes soften as she looks at me. "I see how much work you both put into this place, and I meant it when I said I want to see it succeed. I asked Mr. Pierson if there was anything he wanted us to prepare to help make his stay more enjoyable. He is hoping to get inspired and paint, so I got a list of preferred materials and other things that he would need should inspiration strike. If we keep an easel in the room with spare canvases and paint, it will make it even more of a Painter's Retreat, don't you think?" She looks back at me and raises her eyebrow. I nod and clear my throat while thinking of a way to apologize. "I may not have experience in running a business, but I do have experience in scheduling, accounting, and people-pleasing. I also think I enjoy interior design." She says while looking at the pages on the walls.

I smile. *I'm glad she is at least enjoying herself.* "As for why Pecos is staying in the no-longer-reserved cabin, Mr. Hawke called shortly after and requested a room for him. I wasn't sure how long it would take to fix the Workers Respite cabin, so I made an executive decision." *She is still the same old Sabrina after all, taking care of everything herself.* She crosses her arms and looks out the window, "Yes, I know I don't have that authority either and I'm sorry for over stepping. You both have talked about wanting to turn some of the rooms into lodging for staff, this would give you three a nudge to start fixing the rooms up" she holds her hand up as I start to apologize. "As for the stuff on the walls, Logan asked for my opinions on renovations. I was seeing if wallpaper or paint would look better with the hardwood floors, hence the random colors and pages taped everywhere." She turns and gestures to the walls and floor.

I walk towards her, full of shame now as she puts her hands on her hips "Kris, I have no negative memories of you or us whatsoever. When I was going through some of my darkest days, I looked back fondly at the time we spent together. I was genuinely trying to help and I didn't want what few talents I do have to go to waste. If we're being honest; I was also having fun" she smiles sheepishly while touching the papers taped to the wall.

"I'm so sorry" I blurt out in her moment of pause; her blue eyes shift to look into my gray ones. "I jumped to conclusions and though the worst. You handled everything perfectly; way better than I would have. I know you aren't a spiteful person and that this wasn't about us. I guess I was so caught up in who you were, that I missed who you became" her eyes widen as though she had similar thoughts. "I guess that's true, we don't really know each other for who we are now. From your perspective, your view made perfect sense. You had every right to be cautious, especially when you didn't have all of the info." She walks over and adds, "Thank you for your apology, but I feel like we can add this to our 'misunderstandings' pile." She smiles and pats my hand, letting me know that we are okay. "So tell me about this baby poo green." I say casually while pointing to the ugliest shade of green I have ever seen.

After Sabrina showed me the various wall covering options, we head downstairs for lunch. "About time, I was about to go up and get you two" Logan says with a grin as we enter the kitchen. "Willow filled me in on what happened with Mr. Pierson. I reviewed the paperwork you left on my desk, you keep very detailed records. I must say I'm impressed." He joins his hands together, "We value your money, but please don't leave us. We need you here more than your money" Sabrina laughs as Logan continues to beg her to work here instead of investing. "That is an awful business move. With money, you can hire ten people just like me plus pay for renovations." She pauses before adding, "You guys may need me after all" I shake my head, "So now you're trying to hire her too?" Sabrina laughs as Logan nods.

Luna starts placing big bowls of soup in front of each chair as Mr. Hawke sets a basket of bread on the table. Sabrina and Logan sit next to each other, engrossed in their conversation. Willow brings over a basket of cornbread as Pecos follows with a tray of various spreads for the breads. I finish setting the table as Mr. Hawke silently observes us. "Alright everyone let's get beverages and then take a seat." Logan says as we scurry around for various teas and water.

After everyone takes their seat with their drinks, Logan raises his glass "I want to thank Kristian and Pecos for helping out. Neither of you owe me a thing, yet you both have worked hard on this place with me over the last few months." Logan nods to us and then looks at Willow and Luna. "Thank you, ladies, for the wonderful meal and cleaning the place up. Sabrina, thank you for staying, please teach us your ways." Sabrina laughs as I nod in agreement with Logan. "We also thank you for joining us, Mr. Hawke. We hope you enjoy the food and company" Logan finishes speaking and we all toast before enjoying the soup. "The broth is delicious, and you can really taste the different flavors blending together. I can't wait to see what kind of chili you make" I say after having a couple of spoonsful of the soup. Willow grins as Logan agrees that we should add chili to the menu next week. The rest of the meal is enjoyed by easy conversation and laughter.

CHAPTER TWENTY

~Sabrina~

November 15th

2pm

I wave goodbye to Kris and Willow as they drive off towards town. Luna walks back inside to finish cleaning up, Mr. Hawke watching her intently. He turns to Pecos and starts discussing something in a language I am unfamiliar with. *Now is the perfect time to see if Alex has replied.* I feel my shoulders lower in disappointment as there are no new notifications. *I should call Alex's office, maybe she is working over the weekend. Or maybe she is upset with me.* My thoughts halt as I walk right into a wall. I close my eyes and groan. *Not again.*

Logan reaches out to steady me with a smirk. "Sorry about that, I didn't see you there" I say while looking into his *gorgeous* brown eyes. He chuckles, "Do you ever watch where you're going? You could really hurt yourself one day." He crosses his arms before adding, "People can take this as assault, are the guests safe? Kristian and I don't mind your wandering hands, but how do we know Mr. Hawke is safe? What if he is shirtless for whatever reason? Can you promise to keep your hands to yourself?" I feel my jaw drop in shock. *He isn't serious, is he? Oh no, I did superman punch him two days ago, of course he is worried about Mr. Hawke! I also felt up Pecos before I knew his name.* I look up to see Logan covering his mouth, shoulders shaking slightly.

I narrow my eyes in a mock glare, "You're messing with me, aren't you? You weren't worried about me feeling up Mr. Hawke at all!" I say as I cross my arms and grin. "He may not be, but I am" a deep voice says behind me. I jump and look over my shoulder. I see Pecos standing with his arms crossed next to a shocked Luna. Logan lets loose his laughter as Luna sternly says, "You can't do that Sabrina, that is very inappropriate." I groan and cover my face with my hands. "Depends on what she means by feeling me up, maybe she wants to check for any abnormalities. She could have medical experience" Mr. Hawke adds with an understanding smile. *Alright Earth you can swallow me up any moment now.* I close my eyes and continue to beg mother nature for an escape from this conversation.

"What are your intentions towards my father?" Pecos asks me with furrowed brows. "Completely respectable, I promise. Luna do you need anything?" I ask her in hopes of changing the subject. "It can wait" She replies while tapping her fingers together. *Oh no, now she thinks I am a sexual deviant too.* I groan and cover my face. Mr. Hawke and Logan start laughing as Pecos smiles at me. Luna and I look at each other in confusion. "I told you to be careful, he likes to play tricks" Mr. Hawke winks at me before waving to everyone "Tsaaku mia!" he adds before walking to his truck.

I furrow my brows and cross my arms before asking Pecos why he was messing with me. "Because he likes you" Luna says bluntly while fidgeting. Pecos turns his head and frowns. *I'm sure his heritage is owl, not hawk.* Pecos turns towards her with an unreadable expression on his face. "In what way, little deer?" He asks so low, I almost didn't hear him. "Romantically of course. When boys pick on girls, it's because they secretly want to be their boyfriend. Everyone knows this, there's nothing to be ashamed of." She bites her lip before whispering, "You shouldn't pick on someone if you like them though, that isn't kind of you. I know I wouldn't like that at all." Her jade eyes dart over different parts of his face, as though she were studying a map. *Oh my, this is it. He's going to tell her he likes her!* I keep perfectly still so not to alert them.

Pecos gently lifts a lock of her blonde hair and looks into her eyes, "Then I swear that I will always be kind to you." I suck in a breath at his sweet words, as he rubs her hair between his finger and thumb gently. *It looks so silky.* I make a mental reminder to ask what her haircare line of choice is. "I want you to listen carefully, little deer: I do not like Sabrina in a romantic way. I was teasing her in a brotherly fashion, though she may think of me as more of a stepbrother." Pecos adds as Logan slowly lifts my chin to close my mouth. *That may have been a little true.* "Her advances have all been in vain, I assure you" Pecos smiles down at a fidgeting Luna.

"Thank you, I use LolaVie for my hair by the way. Would you like to try some?" Luna asks while looking at her hair twirled around his finger. His nostrils flare as his gaze lowers to her lips briefly. I grab Logans hand and squeeze it to keep from moving in giddy anticipation. "No, thank you, I have my own routines. I will see you for dinner later, little deer." He says low, almost in a growl. I shiver in anticipation for her. *It sounds like he plans for her to be his dinner.* I continue watching, completely invested in their exchange. "For now, let's go inside. I need to start on the other railings" he drops the lock of hair as they walk towards the B&B, completely oblivious that we have been here the entire time. "Did you see that?" I squeal at Logan as the door closes behind them. "They would make the cutest couple, oh my gosh. It's like watching a cdrama with all the slight touches and small flirtations. I can't handle the cuteness!" I let go of his hand as soon as I realize I am still tightly grasping it. *Not again, curse you wandering hands.* I groan while looking at the smile plastered on his scruffy face, his brown eyes twinkling with amusement.

CHAPTER TWENTY-ONE

~Logan~

November 15th

6:30pm

Once we all sit down at the table. I glance at Kristian before saying, "Things are looking up team. If everyone here works daily to make this place succeed, we will get burnt out. If anyone gets sick, we'll be in trouble for sure." Kristian nods before replying, "We could hire part time help for now and then offer full time once more lodging becomes available. We do need someone besides the three of us that can do electrical, plumbing, and groundskeeping." I nod. "You could offer the same arrangement you offered us. There are several large rooms upstairs. Until the bunkhouse is repaired at least" Luna adds while looking at the vegetables floating in her broth. Pecos turns towards me "After my time at the cabin is up, swap the twin beds in your room for bunk beds to make room for me. I'll stay for a few months as a groundskeeper and repair man." Kristian laughs and makes a comment about Pecos enjoying the local wildlife more than he expected. I snort and continue eating.

"Me staying at the B&B frees up the Workers Respite for another guest. I can work on the cosmetic issues at the B&B, plus the renovation costs for the 6 unavailable cabins." Sabrina says after finishing her cornbread. "If you can get everything back to tip-top shape, I can paint and decorate" She adds and smiles at me. *I still feel as though I'm taking advantage of her.* "What about all the hikes and special additions you added for your stay? Am

105

I the only one upset that you paid for an all-inclusive vacation and instead, you are just giving a stranger money while staying in a shabbier room to work?" The room goes silent as I look between her and Kristian. "Seriously? Don't get me wrong, I see how good you are for this place. I even begged you to stay after your vacation and work here, but it isn't fair to you at all." I shake my head as she frowns. "You could wait until after you have a relaxing vacation before jumping right into work. You haven't even driven the Jeep that you were so excited to rent." I add as I lean back in my chair. Kristian puts his spoon down and frowns at me. Sabrina smiles politely to Willow and Luna "Logan, may I have a word with you outside?" she asks me and I nod.

The chair makes a scraping sound as I stand and follow her to the door. We grab out coats in silence, and I open the door to the cold night air. "What was that about?" She asks calmly, the moonlight casts a blue shine on her raven tresses. *I don't know. I'm scared.* She purses her pink lips and scowls at me as I continue not to answer. I cross my arms and lean against the support beam. "You have been her for only a few days, yet you are already investing in business you barely know anything about. You are out here moving furniture, designing renovations, rescheduling guests while making their stays better, oh and teaching the owners how to talk to said guests." I explain and look back at her. Her lips part as her expression changes to one of shock. *Wait, I'm saying it wrong.*

I exhale slowly before adding, "To me, you are a mystical being sent to make this place better than I could have imagined. I'm terrified that your presence is just a dream. The past year was very tough for me. I kept hitting one issue after another. When my aunt died, I found out at her funeral that she was actually my birth mother. No one ever knew who my father was." Realizing what I let slip I continue, "She left the entire estate to me with money for repairs, but I couldn't find anyone available to work long term. Things kept breaking, crazy summer rains kept creating more setbacks and now early blizzards are keeping guests away. I was ready to quit. Sell the place and move on." I rest my arms on the railing and look up at the stars. "You knocking over my sign was the best thing that's happened to me in a long time. We wouldn't have been able to hire the Hawthorne sisters and Pecos wouldn't have met Luna, which let's face it, that's the main reason he decided to stay." She smiles and nods as I continue, "I wouldn't even have this opportunity if it wasn't for Kristian recognizing you from 10 years ago. Not to mention Mr. Pierson would have probably canceled, so we would have had to deal with that as well. We very well could have just given up if that happened" I exhale slowly, controlling my emotions before they grow into something twisted.

She places her hand on my arm and softly says, "I feel the same way. I was so desperate for change that I sold everything I own and booked a retreat in a climate I had never stayed in. Is this all a bit crazy?" She asks as she waves her hands around, "Absolutely, but I love it. I have lived more in the past few days than I have in the past few years. I don't want that to stop either. No one is promised tomorrow, so I choose to follow my happiness today." She squeezes my hand as I gaze into her crystal-like eyes. "That should be on a t-shirt, maybe we could make it our slogan here." I murmur. "If you will let me stay as just a friend helping out, same as Kristian, then I give it to you freely to use as you wish." She adds with a smile. "Of course, but what's up with you and labels? Guest, friend, investor, what do you want to be and what do we do with the money you already paid?" I ask and she replies with a laugh, "My best friend is a lawyer, it's a habit now to present everything as clearly as possible. That reminds me, you really should have a lawyer review everything and maybe hire an accountant as well. I have met a lot of people that would take advantage of your situation. As far as the money goes, I still want to do what I signed up to do, especially the classes. I also want to stay and help out at the B&B for the month instead of at the cabin." She replies while crossing her arms.

I smirk and lean closer to her "So your idea of presenting

things clearly is to feel up the men and make sexual noises when you eat?" She smacks my arm playfully, "Hey now, if I'm staying as a friend instead of guest or investor, that makes you all fair game. Except Pecos, of course. I have clearly been sister-zoned. Oh! I feel like it's dessert time, let's go get on that." She laughs nervously as I put my arms on railing to either side of her, still giving her room to go if she wishes. "What do you mean by fair game? Does that mean you intend to wait for opportunities to grope Kristian and myself? Are the guests safe at least?" I gaze into her eyes and my lips twitch slightly.

She licks her lips and tilts her chin up, "It means that I have seen the way you two look at me, it's the same way that I look at the both of you" I suck in a breath as she winks at me before ducking under my arm and darting to the door. *Oh now she winks back.* Her laughter brings a smile to my face before I can fully register her words. I shake my head and follow her inside just as Willow sets down two pies. "I knew it was pie time!" Sabrina exclaims as she takes her seat, Kristian hands her a slice soon after. He looks at me with a concerned expression, as though he was asking if everything was alright. I nod back with a smile. *Yea, we're good.* I sit down as everyone enjoys their dessert and easy conversation. "I was told to make pie for as long as Pecos is here" Willow says with a smile. Sabrina raises her glass of water and cheers.

Sabrina laughs as Willow and Kristian become engrossed in a debate of 'which came first, the chicken or the egg?' with Willow staying firm that it was the egg. Pecos shakes his head as Luna furrows her brows. "How could the chicken grow to lay an egg and what would have laid the egg, if not a fully grown hen?" she asks. The phone rings before anyone can answer and I stand quickly. "I'll be right back" I say as Sabrina nods and adds another slice of pie to her plate. "I'm not saving you any" She replies with a grin. Unsure if she is serious or not, I add another slice to my plate before sprinting to my room.

The phone rings again as I rush to the desk inside my room. "It's a great evening at the Retreat, this is Logan speaking, how may I help you?" I answer with a smile, remembering the lessons Sabrina taught us earlier today. *It really does change your tone, fascinating.* "Good evening Logan, my name is Thomas. I'll cut to the chase, I'm looking for something quiet with a dedicated workspace for November 17th through November 26^{th,}. I would like the option to extend to December if needed and I am willing to pay a temporary holding deposit for the extended stay." A tired, deep voice says. I ask him to give me a moment as I look through the schedule, smiling at the weather notes and work orders Sabrina added. *Thank goodness she wanted to stay in the room instead of the cabin.* "We do have one cabin available, let me tell you about it-" I lean back as he cuts me off. "Perfect, book it for Thomas Callahan. Send me an email letting me know of any VIP add-ons not listed on the site, the total price, and your preferred payment method. I will pay in full tonight." He tells me his email address and hangs up quickly.

I poke my head outside and motion for Sabrina and Kristian to come here for a moment. *We need to figure out a proper schedule before emailing Mr. Callahan.* I sit back down at my desk and open the laptop to pull up the Retreat's website. Sabrina walks in with her plate of pie as Kristian follows behind, "What's up boss?" Kristian asks nonchalantly. "Oh no. He can't be your boss, only your friend. Otherwise, he won't be able to date us" Sabrina says casually and takes a bite of pie. I sigh as Kristian gasps theatrically, "My man, you want to ask me out? I am so flattered right now." Kristian raises a hand to his heart. "I heard Pecos sister zoned you, so sorry he won't be able to join" he adds solemnly while looking at Sabrina. "Alright you two, let's pause this since we have a new reservation to discuss" I say with a low chuckle.

Kristian walks over to his desk and rolls his chair over for Sabrina before pulling over the spare chair folded by the dresser. I go over the phone call with Mr. Callahan and lean forward, "I think the Worker's Respite would be perfect for him since Sabrina will be staying at the B&B. We need to go over what the weather would permit us to do in regard to hikes or picnics." Sabrina pulls out her phone and says, "It looks like the 17th-19th, and 23rd- 26th will all be optimal weather for anything outdoors. You can offer guided hikes, chef prepared picnics, local tours, and fishing on those days. We will need to prepare for the snow expected on the 20th-22nd. Logan, you need to make sure we are on the plower's schedule, unless you want to try and catch another investor?" She looks at me as Kristian throws his head back and laughs. I shake my head and continue typing.

Kristian leans back in his chair, "Tomorrow is Sunday, the sisters have the day off and will be in town most of the day. I already paid them in advance should they need to get anything while they're out. Pecos and I will be working on the Hideaway during that time. It's the cabin towards the edge of the wood line in the back" Kristian adds after noticing Sabrina's look of confusion. "Sabrina, can you knock out renovation cost sheets for the Hideaway and the Yellow room upstairs? I think the Yellow room would be perfect for Pecos later. After he leaves it can be used for future staff." I ask as Kristian holds out his hand. She grins and hands him her now empty pie plate. "I haven't seen the Hideaway yet, but I've already looked at the Yellow room. I typed everything up earlier. Repairs, new wallpaper, furniture, and materials would total around $4,200." She adds after flipping through the stack of papers on my desk. "That's presuming we do the work ourselves. Here you go." She pulls out a paper and hands it to me. "Wow. You listed everything down to the cost of the screws, impressive." I pause to review the costs again before adding, "This is doable. I would like to rotate renovations between cabins and rooms to ensure we have enough staff on hand." Sabrina grins as I add on to Mr. Callahans email.

A notification pops up for a reservation request. I review the request while Kristian and Sabrina discuss the Hideaway. *Where in the world is it morning right now?* I run my hand through my hair and lean back as I re-read the email. "Hey Kristian, didn't the

Hideaway have a cracked tub liner? What if we just take out the whole thing and add a clawfoot soaking tub?" I ask. He frowns, "You're the licensed plumber, you tell me. I don't mind the extra work, but why a soaking tub?" He replies as Sabrina claps her hands together in excitement, "I would very much like to soak in a clawfoot tub" she adds. I laugh and remind her there is a hot tub right outside whenever she wants to use it. "Yeah but it's not the same" she huffs.

I prop an elbow on the desk before saying, "This is the email I just got. 'Good morning. I'm emailing in hopes of making a reservation for November 30th - December 6th for one adult named Ripley Baker with no pets. A cabin with a clawfoot soaking tub is preferred. I would like to add the daily meals package along with a guided waterfall hike. Please let me know how much in total and when check in/check out is. Ripley B.' The Hideaway would be perfect since it needs a new tub anyway." He nods and we continue discussing the renovation plans before Sabrina excuses herself to go shower. After she closes the door, Kristian turns to me before saying, "What did she mean by 'If he's the boss then he can't date us'? What did you two talk about?" he wiggles his eyebrows and grins, his gray eyes shining with mischief. *That didn't take long.*

CHAPTER TWENTY-TWO

~Sabrina~

November 17th
8:30am
Two days later

After breakfast, everyone moves to the living room to go over the schedule. "Sabrina, why don't you start us off?" Logan asks and I nod. "Mr. Jenkins will be stopping by later to drop off some pastries. He will be bringing information pamphlets from various shops around town as well for us to keep in the rooms for guests. Logan, don't forget to preorder any desserts you don't want to make have to make here for the holiday banquet in a few weeks. We also should work on a guest list for that this week." Logan nods and I look around. "Pecos will get a ride back to town with Mr. Jenkins to pick up the furniture we ordered a few days ago. Including our lovely new clawfoot tub and toilet Mr. Hawke *just so happened* to have on hand. Logan and Kris will be working on the Hideaway in preparation for that." They grin as I continue, "After Pecos drops off the furniture, the other driver will return the truck. Pecos will stay here to work on the Yellow room. Luna will be on top of cleaning and double checking that everything is ready for Mr. Callahan's arrival at 6pm. Mr. Callahan requested all meals to be delivered to his cabin daily. Willow will be making snacks and meal prepping while waiting for a few other deliveries to arrive." I turn to Willow and smile. "When I'm not helping with whatever anyone needs, I will be working on removing the wallpaper in the rooms upstairs. Does anyone have any questions or am I forgetting anything?" Pecos murmurs that I should make sure to keep my hands off the guest, as everyone erupts in laughter.

Everyone moves towards their tasks as Luna walks over to me with a bucket. "Here are some gloves, a scraper, spray bottles, and other stuff you may need. I'll bring snacks by every few hours and check if you need anything." She leans in and whispers, "Sometimes when I am deep in thought or working hard, I forget to do anything else too." She hands me the bucket and reminds me that I can call her if I change my mind. "I really do enjoy this" I reply easily. *I think I have fallen in love with renovating and decorating.* Pecos frowns as Willow brushes past him. "Don't forget about tonight. Logan is making something special for dinner, so be washed up and ready to eat by 6pm. I'll bring some to Mr. Callahan after he checks in." She says before walking towards the kitchen. *Did something happen between Willow and Pecos? Not your concern right now, Sabrina.* I clear my mind to focus on my current tasks.

5:30pm

I moan as the warm water flows over my aching shoulders. My head falling forward as I arch my back into the spray. *Who knew taking off wallpaper was so difficult? I finished three different rooms before Luna and I went to set up the cabin for Mr. Callahan.* I grin as the feeling of accomplishment flows through me. *It feels better than when we celebrated a successful month at the **place that shan't be named**.* Logan pulled me to the side an hour ago to remind me that tonight was supposed to be my 'picnic under the stars' package for the meteor shower. Since Mr. Callahan didn't add the package, Logan would be staying back in case anyone needed anything. Kris would be taking me instead. *Hopefully, he thought about my suggestion to invite Luna and Pecos. It would be nice to catch up with Kris though.* After my shower, I change into a new pair of jeans and one of the cozy sweaters that arrived earlier. The dark red accenting my hair beautifully. I apply a thin swipe of 'champagne shimmer' to my eyelids with a touch of mascara to complete the look. My towel-dried wavy tresses barely touch my shoulders as I put on a pair of soft black socks. *I forgot about the clothes I ordered; I owe Alex another apology for her 'over prepping'.* I walk over to the half open boxes and work on unpacking them. *I'll wash the other stuff before I wear it, but this sweater is perfect for tonight.* After removing the tags, I looked at the soft sweaters, pants, pj sets, socks, and other stuff piled high atop the bed. I grab the pile and toss them into the laundry basket for Luna to wash later.

I sit down at the white desk by the window and open my laptop to check for new emails. *Looks like mostly junk, spam, nothing important, and still nothing from Alex. I'm starting to get worried.* I send a quick text to the group chat and ask if anyone has heard from Daddy lately. I remind myself that she is a very busy hot shot lawyer, and that I am probably overreacting. I close my laptop as I hear a knock at my door outside. I walk over to the door and open it to see Luna fidgeting anxiously. "Logan asked me to go with you tonight as a 'guest' and take notes on how the men do as guides." She says before I can welcome her in. "Hey Luna, come on in." I smile while stepping to the side. *So, he is playing matchmaker after all!* I inwardly squeal at Logan's idea. *I know just how to help.* I feel my lips part in a big grin as I try to reign in my excitement.

Luna walks in after a moment and stands by the window. "I have never been a guest anywhere, could you teach me?" She says while looking around the room. *She is so similar to Layla, I should see if I can find a way to introduce them.* "Absolutely! I can also loan you some 'guest clothes' if you'd like as well." *Please let me play dress up with you, I've always wanted a little sister.* I shake my head and remind myself she is not a doll. She smiles and nods, "Yes please. That would be very helpful. Logan said that everyone going will need to meet at the B&B by 9pm. I like white, pastel pink, and baby blue. I don't like make-up or synthetic fragrances, but I do like sparkly things. Like a dragon." She adds while tapping her fingers together by her sides.

The sweater dress in many colors! "I have the perfect dress in each of those colors! Try them on and see which one you like."

I walk over to the closet and grab the three dresses. "Would you be alright with a little bit of shimmer eyeshadow? If so, come by around 8:30pm and I can help you with it." I ask while hanging the dresses in the bathroom. She nods and walks into the bathroom, closing the door softly behind her. I grin and grab the purple sweater dress. I throw it on over my black jeans as she comes out in the light pink version, also wearing her white jeans underneath. *I was right, she has a nice figure under those baggy clothes.* I smile as she looks in the mirror and back at me, "This is *really* soft. I don't think I've ever liked a dress before." Luna says softly while rubbing her arms, clearly in love with cashmere now. *I know exactly what you mean.*

I look at our reflections in the mirror, and I smile. *The boys don't stand a chance.* "I think you should keep that dress, it looks way better on you. I really don't need so many shades of one dress." Even after my explanation, she shakes her head. "I can't take this, it feels really expensive." She says meekly as she walks back into the bathroom. I walk closer to the door so she can hear me, "Please take it. I really don't have room for so many clothes here. I forgot how much I ordered while sitting at the airport. I don't know if you noticed, but the hamper can't even close with all of it" I gesture to the overfull hamper as though she can see me. She opens the door and looks at the hamper. "I will wash those in just a bit" she closes the door and I laugh. "That wasn't the point Luna" I pick up my tossed sweater and change, already eager to see what was for dinner.

CHAPTER TWENTY-THREE

~Kristian~

November 17th
8:30pm

I cover my mouth as Pecos almost snaps his neck with a double take at Luna. She slowly walks down the stairs, oblivious to his reaction. Her blonde hair was pinned back on the sides, soft curls bouncing with each step. She's wearing a peach-colored sweater with pale blue jeans. Pecos stands and walks to her in long strides, looking at her as though she were clothed in regality. He raises his arm in an escort fashion, and she looks at it with an unreadable expression. She glances at Logan as I hold up my arm and he places his hand on it. She slowly raises her hand and touches Pecos's arm. He smiles at her, his gaze softening as he murmurs something to her. She blushes and shakes her head. "I'm sorry, I'm not ready yet. I have to go to Sabrina's room first" Pecos smiles and escorts her to Sabrina's door before walking back towards Logan and myself.

He pauses and raises his brow at us, "What are you two doing?" he asks while looking at Logan's hand on my arm. "Deeping the bromance, would you like to join?" I ask as Logan laughs. Pecos shakes his head, "I already told you, been there, done that, no thank you." Logan removes his hand and grins. "Willow is doing laundry upstairs and will stay back in case anyone needs anything. The sites are already set up with coolers full of water and cold apps. Inside the bags on the counter, you will find thermoses of hot cocoa, chili, Cornish pies, thermal blankets, and a few other goodies." Logan grins before continuing, "I set plenty of firewood out there and the telescope is already aligned and in the gazebo. Don't forget this is practice for guided hikes and guest safety. I've already given the ladies a few ideas for 'events' that could very well happen in the future." I nod before adding, "We need to be prepared for anything, especially if we have guests with no outdoor experience". *I wonder if he knows Sabrina and I met at a LARPing event.* My mind drifts back to memories of our first meeting. *Bri's long black hair pinned back with tiny braids, as her eyes scanned the forest for me. Her black and purple archer outfit matched her bow perfectly.* I shake my head and grin, "I have to admit I'm a bit excited to see what he has planned." I whisper to Pecos. *Especially now that Luna and Pecos have joined.*

Logan pulls out a barstool and sits down, facing Sabrina's room. "Mr. Callahan wants privacy, so let's make sure to keep it down until you get to the gazebo. I'll head out soon to light the lanterns and start the fires. Again, Sabrina and Luna are playing the role of *guests,* and you are their *guides.* They will be reporting on how well you explain things, handle situations, and overall safety. The best guide will get to pick *any* of the non-reserved cabins, or *any* non-reserved room at the B&B for their residence during their stay here. After we renovate it of course." He grins as Pecos and I look at each other. *That includes the main suite upstairs and the Waterfall cabin.* "If you decide to move on from this place, simply give it back in decent condition, no worries" He adds with an easy-going smile. "Agreed" we say in unison, furrowing our brows at each other. "I thought you only wanted to fix a few things, now you want to stay?" I ask Pecos with a smirk. "You know I don't share my father's vision of living with the family forever." He replies with an unreadable expression.

Pecos and I shake hands as the door to Sabrina's room opens. I look over to see Sabrina and Luna walking out looking like twins, but opposite. Sabrina's dark purple sweater dress and black leggings make her blue eyes pop. Her red lips part slightly as she catches me looking at her. *She looks beautiful.* I smile at her and look towards Luna, who had changed into a light pink version of Sabrina's dress. Her white leggings had shimmering snowflakes. *Cute, but I hope they don't get cold.* Logan stands and greets them, "Welcome Ms. Eldwin and Ms. Hawthorne. These gentlemen are Pecos Hawke and Kristian Graham. They will be your guides for this evening. They will also be giving you a bit of information on what to expect tonight, as well as safety precautions." Logan grabs his coat and adds, "I will leave Mr. Graham to answer any questions you have." Luna looks at me and raises her hand. I nod to her. "Which came first, the chicken or the egg?" she asks with a serious expression. Logan's laughter echos from outside as he closes the door behind him.

~Pecos~

After Kris's Q&A, he went over the plan for tonight and safety tips. *Logan should have enough of a head start now.* "Let's go ahead and start heading towards the gazebo. That way we have time to set up and relax before the meteor shower" I say while looking at Kris. He nods in agreement as we move towards the bags on the counter. "I'm hungry, is there anything to snack on?" Sabrina asks while looking at her glossy black nails. Kris laughs and grabs the bags off the counter, handing me one in the process. "Yes ma'am, the kitchen has a variety of snacks, what are you in the mood for?" He asks her as she shrugs nonchalantly. *So, she is playing the difficult guest.* I turn towards Lunabella and watch as she walks down the hallway, looking at the pictures lining the walls. *And what role will you be playing, I wonder.*

I walk over as she stops in front of a photograph of a boy perched high in the treetops. "That was taken from the balcony of the Waterfall cabin by the late Dana Hale." I explain as she reaches out to touch the frame. She pulls back before making contact. "Weren't you afraid you would fall?" she asks me, her jade eyes moving to the other pictures. "What makes you think the boy in the photo is me?" I ask after a moment. "You stand the same, as though you are untouchable. Your stance is fearless." she says without hesitation. "Alright, is everyone ready?" Kris asks with an amused expression as he and Sabrina walk down the hall. "Oh, I almost forgot!" Sabrina says before rushing back to her room. Lunabella puts on her pinky puffy coat; the handsewn snowflakes on the inner liner shimmer with the movement.

Sabrina walks out holding a long white coat, "Luna, this is for you. I have one in black too. I feel like it will complete our look tonight if we wear them. What do you think? They are *extremely* resistant to stains and are very warm." She holds up the coat for Lunabella to see. She nods after thinking it over. "Thank you. I will take very good care of it" she replies with a smile. I raise my hands to help with her coat as she flinches before stepping back. She smiles sheepishly and takes her coat off quickly and hangs it up. "Are you alright?" I ask softly while Sabrina holds the coat up for Lunabella to slip on. "Yes. I'm ready now" she replies while turning to Kris. He smiles and grabs his bag before opening the door. Sabrina goes after him with a concerned look pointed at Lunabella. I sling my backpack over my shoulder and follow Lunabella onto the porch, locking the door behind me. *I'll drop it for now, little deer.*

Gasps alert me and I turn towards our guests. "Oh wow, when did this happen?" Sabrina says as she follows Kris down the lantern lit stairs. "All of the previous owners of this place had done special touches for their guests; Logan is no different from them in that regard. He wants to create that same magic. The Retreat has always been a place where people could come to forget their struggles for a moment" Kris replied while looking at the lanterns placed along the path. He goes on about the history of the Retreat as I hold my hand out to Lunabella, who is tapping her gloved fingers together at the top of the stairs. "I have a depth perception problem so I can't tell where the steps are in the shadows" She explains nervously. "I'll be sure to tell Logan to add more lighting along the stairs" I reply while turning on the flashlight on my belt, illuminating the area at our feet. She murmurs a quick thank you as we walk down the stairs.

Once we start along the lit path, Kris moves on to discuss the area's history. Sabrina asks if any pirates stayed in the area and he says no with a laugh. "Actually, quite a bit of people would seek refuge in the mountains. It is quite possible pirates were amongst them" Lunabella adds while walking awkwardly beside me. *She is very smart.* "That is right, little deer. How-" a small, gloved hand covers my mouth before I can ask how she knew that. "Shhhhh! No nicknames. You don't know me remember?" her eyes briefly lock with mine and I smile against her palm. I gently place my hand over hers and lower it. "Alright, but I *am* allowed to give nicknames to guests. Would you prefer I give you a new one for when you are playing 'guest'? Is there anything you had in mind?" I ask in a lower tone. She looks at various features of my face before answering. "I want to be a temptress, like Sabrina, so something bold." I chuckle "Sabrina is not a temptress, and I do not think bold suits you." *Wrong choice of words.* I mentally groan as she narrows her eyes at me. "I think bold could suit me very well, Mr. Hawke." Lunabella adds after a moment. She turns and follows Sabrina as I groan. *Great job Mr. Hawke.* I frown and keep up the pace.

A few minutes later

Sabrina sighs and asks if we are there yet and grumbles. "We have been walking around following these lamps forever, I'm hungry. I signed up to see rocks flying across the sky, not a dimly lit nature hike with Ken over here" she points towards Kris and his lips twitch. *Don't laugh.* I turn around as though I were checking for wildlife, steeling my resolve with an exhale. Lunabella leans towards me and whispers, "Are we going the right way?" I look at her and nod. "Yes, Ms. Lunabella. I assure you, Mr. Graham knows this land like the back of his hand, almost as well as I do." She nods and we continue down the path behind Sabrina and Kristian. *She has barely said a word to me since our 'bold' discussion. I didn't mean to insult her.* I adjust the bag on my shoulder and stop. *Of course!* I pull the bag off my back and look through it as I whistle to Kris to stop. Lunabella flinches and fidgets next to Sabrina. *Sudden movements and loud noises startle her. I will need to be more careful.* I frown and continue to dig through the bag.

After pulling the blue thermos out, I ask "Would anyone like to take a break for some hot chocolate? There are a few logs up ahead we can rest on." Lunabella nods eagerly as Kris shakes his head. *Point to Pecos.* I smile at my small victory as Sabrina motions for Lunabella to join her up ahead. I feel my lips shift downwards as Lunabella smiles and walks faster to meet her friend. "Point to Sabrina" Kris says to me with a knowing smile before trotting off after the ladies. I sigh and walk over to the logs and set out a blanket over the long one.

Kris pulls out his green thermos and pours a cup of hot cocoa, "Here you go" he says while handing Sabrina a cup. She smiles and thanks him before sitting on the blanket covered log. I pull the blue thermos out of my bag and pour a cup for Lunabella. "Woul-" I turn to give it to her, but Sabrina is already handing her another cup from Kris. Lunabella smiles and sits next to Sabrina. "This is delicious, just what I needed." She says while looking up at the stars. I walk over and take Kris's cocoa as he grins at me, "Looks like it's my turn" I say before taking a big gulp. It burns, but I don't let it show as I start talking about the stories in the stars. He chuckles and pulls out another cup from my bag before pouring himself another cup.

CHAPTER TWENTY-FOUR

~Sabrina~

November 17th

9pm

As we walk into the clearing, I see a bonfire set up with stone seats spread around it. A short distance from it lies a huge stone table in an odd shape with logs set around it. From there, lanterns light a path to a big gazebo with a telescope inside "This is beautiful" Luna claps her hands together and grins as she looks around. "Would you like to see the stars through the nightscopes? I have two pair in my bag since the telescope is already set up for the shower later" Pecos asks her. She nods and they walk to the gazebo, their voices fading out slowly. "What about you, Ms. Eldwin? Want to go stargazing with them? I have nightscopes you can use as well." Kris says beside me while looking up at the stars. *No, I want them to have some privacy so their love can blossom.* I crinkle my nose at my inability to stay out of people's business. "No thank you" I reply as I walk over to one of the stones by the fire to sit down. *Besides, it's my job to be difficult tonight, sorry Kris.*

Kris walks past me towards the table. *With his blonde hair glowing in the firelight, he looks almost like a ghost.* He walks over to a cooler near the table and asks me if I'd like anything to drink or eat. "I do love snacks" I say as I stand and walk over to him. I look down and see bowls of cut fruit, various cheeses, a few bottles of wine, chocolates, and personal Caesar salads. "Wow, this all looks amazing, can I have some of everything?"

I ask as my stomach tightens in anticipation. He chuckles and says he will set everything up. I walk back to the fire and sit down, I casually glance at Luna as Pecos points in the sky and leans closer to tell her something. I tilt my head up to look at the stars, enjoying the sounds of the fire crackling in front of me. *It's so beautiful here, and peaceful too.* I close my eyes, enjoying the sounds of nature.

The sound of a sharp whistle pulls me from my relaxed state, and my eyes snap open. *When did I close my eyes?* My head swivels to pinpoint where the noise came from. Kris grins from the table and waves at me before reaching into his coat pocket. He pulls out a small black rectangle and I hear Pecos's distorted voice. Kris frowns and replies, "I was wondering if you and Ms. Hawthorne would like some snacks since we have a bit of time before the shower." Kris says into the walkie as I look at the beautiful assortment of food spread across the table. "We will be over soon. Let's use these instead of whistling from now on." Pecos says, more clear this time. I smile knowing it probably startled Luna too. *He is so considerate of her, I can't wait to see how this plays out.* I grin excitedly as Kris stares at me.

Kris put the walkie back in his pocket and asks if I would like anything to drink. I nod, "The red wine please, do you know if it is sweet?" Kris says it is a full bodied, nutty wine. I crinkle my nose and look down. "I didn't know you preferred red now." He says softly while holding the bottle. "I'm sorry Mr. Graham, I believe you have me confused with someone else. I have never seen you before this evening." I say while tilting my chin up. He laughs and reaches back into the cooler, digging through the ice to the bottom before pulling out a bottle of familiar peach wine. "How unfortunate then. I brought this to share with a friend, but I must have been mistaken. This was a good friend of mine's favorite wine, I remember she would buy it by the case because she was worried they would close the vineyard down. Unfortunately, she was right and it did close." His eyes shine with mischief as my jaw drops. "Where did you find this? I have looked all over the country for this." I take the bottle and hug it as he chuckles and holds out the cork screw.

I hand him back the bottle for him to open as I sit down at the stone table. He explains that he bought quite a few cases at a deep discount when they sold their vineyard years ago. He hands me the glass and I inhale the sweet peach aroma, closing my eyes as the flashbacks come in waves. *Instead of capturing the intruder for my Queen, I ended up captured by him and drinking wine in a glamping tent. I was shocked at his lavish lifestyle in the middle of a LARPing event. He event bought the title of Duke to support it. At least it was for charity. I miss having fun like that. I also miss that giant bed with black sheets.* "It smells even better than I remember" I add before taking a sip. I release a slow moan of pure bliss at the zero-percent sour wine delighting my tastebuds right now. After I swallow and open my eyes, I notice Lunabella watching me curiously as Pecos shakes his head while setting his bag down. "Lunabella Hawthorne, you simply must try this *delicious* wine" I say in my most posh voice. She giggles and nods her head while sitting down. "Mr. Graham, a glass for my friend here" I say while waving at Kris who is standing *maybe* six feet away from me. He chuckles and pulls out another glass.

Pecos asks Luna which snacks she would prefer and she points to my plate. "I think I want to try a little of each, to see what I like of course." She says while imitating my posh voice. I raise my glass to my lips and smile. Kris hands her a glass of wine, "Let me know if you ladies need anything. We have about 30 minutes until the shower" he says before walking over to Pecos. Luna thanks him and sips the wine, grinning instantly. "This is amazing. I've never had such a yummy wine!" she exclaims while sipping more. I laugh, knowing how smooth it tastes. We chat about beautiful scenery and other small topics. "Lunabella my dear, what do you think of our *fine* guides this evening?" I say after a while, continuing my wine-induced posh persona. She pauses a moment, "They need some practice and seem nervous. The paths could be lit more, but they seem to be knowledgeable and-" I lean over and whisper, "I am talking about their looks, miss ma'am." I sip my wine and look around as

124

she processes my words.

Her eyes widen and she takes a bigger gulp. *She's almost done with her glass. Time really flies when you're having fun.* I raise my glass to finish the last of my wine as she replies, "I very much want to lick that one" as she points to Pecos. Peach wine is spewed from my lips in a majestic arc. Luna jumps and stands back as Pecos rushes over to hand me a towel. I start laughing as I register her words. "What on earth happened?" Kris asks Luna as I take the towel from Pecos and start patting myself dry. "Sabrina asked how I thought you two were doing tonight and I sai-" I quickly put my hand over her mouth before she can embarrass herself. "Oh no you don't mister, you aren't finding out about our secret review for Logan. Don't fall for their tricks Luna, it's a trap" I say with my lips twitching as I struggle not to think about what she said earlier. She furrows her brows in determination before nodding her head in agreement.

Pecos stays quiet as he sets the plate for Luna on the table. *Did he hear or did he not hear? That is the question.* I mull it over as Kris tries to deny any nefarious digging on his part. Luna effectively going into silent mode to protect 'the secret review'. I shake my head and give Luna a cracker with cheese on it. "We need to make sure we eat and drink water so we don't get a hangover." I remind us as Kris walks over to the fire with Pecos. She nods and pulls the plate closer to her, so she doesn't drop crumbs on the ground. *That's right, we don't want to attract any wildlife.* I think back to Kris's safety brief earlier and smile, "I am having such a great night, another glass please, Mr. Graham." Luna nods in agreement and finishes off her glass. "Will you keep it in the glass this time?" Pecos murmurs and I snort. He brings the bottle over to refill our glasses. Pecos grabs a bottle of water and walks over to sit across from Luna. Kris sits next to him after placing the wine bottle back in the cooler.

As everyone settles into easy conversations, we lose track of time. Kris's watch alarm goes off letting us know it's time to go to the gazebo to watch the meteor shower. Lunabella stands awkwardly and then straightens once she notices me watching her. "Are you alright?" I stand in front of her in case she needs to hold on to me as she replies, "I read on the plane that if your body isn't used to a higher elevation, you can feel the effects of alcohol more intensely. I forgot about that". I glance over at Pecos with his back to us and whisper, "Do you want us to watch the shower from here? We don't have to walk over there." She shakes her head and tells me she's got it. *Wait, I have an idea for training.* I grin at my new plan and lean over to whisper, "Instead of the scenario where a guest has an allergy, what if we improvise and do a drunk guest scenario instead?" Her eyes widen and she nods with a smile before sitting down. "Don't lick Pecos!" I sternly whisper to her. She pouts as I hold in my laugh.

CHAPTER TWENTY-FIVE

~Kristian~
10pm

Upon realizing our guests were 'drunk', Pecos and I carefully escorted them to the gazebo for the meteor shower. *Guests drinking too much does seem risky, maybe we should bring small personal bottles or cans in the future. It's a good thing we brought coffee.* After the shower, we sat and drank coffee for a while as we talked amongst ourselves. Before long, Sabrina mentions it's been *ages* since she last ate. *Pecos is already setting up the food woman.* I shake my head and lead them back to the table. After dropping them off with Pecos, I walk back to clean up the gazebo and pack up the telescope. I hear the echos of laughter and I smile. *When was the last time any of us laughed like this? Looks like we just needed a bonfire, good company, and snacks to find our happiness again.* I chuckle as I pick up the pace, eager to return to my friends.

As I walk back to the table, I hear the women start laughing again. "What did I miss?" I ask before I sit down. "Sabrina tried the chili and started sounding like a por-" Luna stops talking as Sabrina's hand covers her mouth. I laugh and Pecos's lips twitch, "You would think she would still remember the taste since we had it at first dinner" he says as the table erupts in laughter. "Alright, it's been almost an hour. Another glass Mr. Graham, that was our deal." Sabrina says while holding her glass in the air. *She does seem fine now, and it has been almost an hour.* I pour a glass of peach wine and hand it to her. Luna holds up her glass as though to ask for more. Before she can speak, Pecos asks if anyone wants s'mores later. She turns her head so fast, I worry she may be part owl too. I chuckle as she sets her glass down and take another bite instead. Sabrina just raises her hand as she sips her wine and I grin. *I'm glad she is still the same old Bri.* The table settles into a peaceful silence as we all enjoy our second dinner.

Sabrina groans and rubs her stomach after we move to sit by the fire. Pecos adds another log as I set up the s'mores station on one of the stone seats. "You ate too much, didn't you Ms. Eldwin?" I ask with a chuckle. "Oh, hush you, with your delicious snacks. Look at you! You're making more delicious snacks right now!" She exclaims while pointing at me. Pecos chuckles as he and Luna sit next Sabrina. Sabrina leans over to Luna and whispers something to her. Luna shakes her head with an apologetic look. "Do you want an antacid? I have some in my bag" Sabrina shakes her head. "Is everything alright?" Pecos asks with concern. "She needs to go to the bathroom" Luna replies nonchalantly.

Sabrina laughs, "Well, yes." I look at her and motion behind me. "I'm not going in the woods. I can wait Kris." she adds hastily. *I didn't mean the woods, I meant we should head back.* I chuckle as Luna frowns and explains that it isn't good to hold it in. "Mr. Graham can take you back to B&B and then you can either stay there or come back. I didn't drink anymore or eat much so, I don't have to po-" Sabrina jumps up, interrupting her to say, "That sounds like a great idea. Grab your bag Mr. Graham, unless you have a restroom with plumbing out here of course." Sabrina stands and starts walking towards the path as I scramble to gather our things. "Wait! Sabrina, don't go off by yourself!" I yell while stuffing our things into my backpack. Pecos hands me the thermos while forcing a straight face. "I don't think she is waiting" Luna says while putting a marshmallow on her skewer. "I mutter under my breath as Pecos tells me he will take care of the rest. I nod and sling the bag on my back before I trot after Sabrina.

~Pecos~

My lips twitch as I watch Kris trot after Sabrina. *I really hope she makes it.* I turn to face Lunabella, and I feel a pang in my chest. The firelight surrounds her in an ethereal glow, making her appear as though she were a snow fairy. *She looks as though she was just enjoying an evening out amongst the mortals, enjoying their marshmallow offerings.* Her small cascading snowflake earrings flicker in the firelight as she turns her head towards me. "Would you like a toasted marshmallow?" she asks while lifting her skewer away from the fire. "I would love one, Ms. Hawthorne, thank you." I walk towards her as she crinkles her nose. She hands me her skewer with a perfectly roasted marshmallow on it. *Not a single black spot, impressive.* "Here you go, *Mr. Hawke.*" She says with a mischievous smile. *Still don't like being called that.* I furrow my brows as I add chocolate on top of my graham crackers. "Are you feeling better, Ms. Hawthorne?" I ask before taking a bite. "I was never feeling bad, but I'm no longer feeling inebriated if that is what you are referring to." she replies curtly. *I want to hear her say my name.* "What if we use our first names as our nicknames?" I ask as she holds her skewer over the fire. "I would like that." She replies with a gentle curve to her lips.

I glance over as she eats the marshmallow off her skewer, smiling and wiggling with her eyes closed. I can't stop the smile forming on my face as I offer the bag to her, "You don't have to eat the chocolate or graham crackers if you don't want to". She opens her eyes and looks at the stars while nodding. "Thank you. I don't like graham crackers, and the chocolate is very messy." she adds while crinkling her nose again. She looks at me briefly before reaching into the bag. Her fingers brush against mine and she jerks her hand back, dropping the marshmallow back into the bag. I soften my gaze and pick up another one, placing it on her skewer as she fidgets. "I won't push it, but I'm here if you want to talk about it" I say softly. She shakes her head and waves her hands, "No, no, it's nothing like that. I'm just nervous and unused to physical contact. Even hugs overwhelm me." She adds quietly as though she was embarrassed. I exhale in relief. *I thought something terrible had happened to you.*

"There is nothing wrong with not wanting to be touched." I say after a moment. She shakes her head, "That isn't what I said. I never said I didn't *want* it. I said I'm not *used* to it. I very much dream of doing things the 'romantic' way. I also love haunted houses, but no one will ever take me because they think it's too scary for me. I'm a grown woman; I shouldn't have to as-" She closes her mouth and looks at the fire. *Don't stop now little deer, tell me more about you.* I add a marshmallow to my skewer, "The only normal that should matter, is what is normal to *you*. Your normal could be physically reading a 200 page book in thirty minutes while still being able to recite it the next day. That wouldn't be my normal at all. My normal would be *listening* to a book while I build something and maybe remember half of the characters by the time I finish listening to it for the 3rd time." I say, smiling as her lips twitch upwards. "I'm sure your sister wouldn't mind helping you practice. Sabrina is a hugger, so she would probably love to help too" I add as she starts tapping her fingers together. "This is bad" she says while shaking her head. "What do you mean? Did I do something wrong?" I reply with concern. *Did I overstep?* "It's on fire" she replies while pointing to my skewer. I look at the marshmallow and shake it off into the fire with a frown as she stands.

Lunabella shakes her head, "I don't want to touch people platonically" she bites her lip and shakes her head again. "That's not what- I didn't mean-" I stand and hold my hand palm up in front of her, her jade eyes searching my dark ones for a moment before looking away. "Hover your hand above mine." She frowns and I add "Don't lower it until we touch, hover just above my hand instead. Just get used to the heat from my hand before worrying about the pressure from actual touch." I say gently. She bites her lip and slowly lowers her hand about an inch above mine. "Don't move it to scare me, okay?" she says nervously and I nod. *Her hand is so small.* I look at her face and see a look of pure wonder across her face. "Has no one done this for you?" I

130

ask, concern filling my voice. She shakes her head slowly. I frown as I look up to the sky. *No more will you be unheard and unseen. I promise you this, little deer.* We stay like this in silence, enjoying the peaceful moment.

Twigs snapping in the distance alert me and I rise slowly. Lunabella does the same as we look towards the moving shadow on path back to the B&B. Logan waves to us as he walks closer and I hear Lunabella exhale. "Sabrina was right, you all do need bells." She says as I smile and add marshmallows on the skewers, handing them out once Logan reaches us. "How was the meteor shower?" He asks while taking a skewer. "Amazing. We made wishes, and they told us stories about the stars. I'm very grateful to have been here" Lunabella says, glancing in my direction with the last part. "Yes, it has been a very nice evening." I add as I look back at her. *Very, nice indeed.*

Logan smiles and lifts his blackened marshmallow before blowing it out. Lunabella makes a face of absolute horror as Logan eats the charred sugar before saying, "Excellent, I ran into Kristian and Sabrina on the way here. They said they had a good time too. I can get your reports tomorrow, so enjoy the rest of the night as yourselves." He sits down and adds another marshmallow to his skewer as Lunabella watches him in mute fascination. He nods to me, "I believe Kristian wanted to soak his leg in the hot tub if you want to join him later." Lunabella looks at me with her nostrils flaring slightly. *Interesting, does the little deer want to see me shirtless?* "I do miss the hot springs" I murmur and nod my head. "I might as well pop in if you're going" He says while rubbing his stubble. I narrow my eyes and ask him, "Did you clean up your beard?" Lunabella snaps her fingers together before exclaiming, "That's what's different! Logan wanted to look pretty tonight too" She grins and I feel my lips twitch. "Why yes I did, Ms. Luna." He replies with a laugh.

CHAPTER TWENTY-SIX

~Sabrina~
Earlier

Oh no, please no. I grab my stomach and grimace as Kris yells at me not to go on my own. I brush him off and continue down the path, determined to not poop myself on my first night stargazing in over a decade. *Why did you eat so much chili, Sabrina? Now you can't end the perfect night with the perfect s'more. Ugh!* I continue berating myself until I hear someone trotting after me. "Sabrina! Why did you walk off like that? The woods are dangerous." He says sternly, his gray eyes almost glowing silver in the light of the lanterns. "Walk and talk, Kris." I walk a little faster before looking over my shoulder. "You can fuss at me while we walk Mr. Graham." I add more politely, continuing down the path as my guts rearrange themselves. *Please hurry.* I start to weigh the risks of running and possibly slipping on ice. *Wait, that's perfect. If I get a good running start I can slide down to the B&B, penguin style.* The gurgle in my belly tells me I would end up a self-propelled rocket if I tried it.

Kris catches up quickly before he put his hand on my arm, gently but firmly stalling me. He looks down at me with a frown. "This is serious. You could have put yourself in a dangerous position-" I grab his hand and pull him down the path with me as I reply, "I'm going to put YOU in a dangerous position if you don't hurry up and get me to a bathroom." I drag him along for a moment before he starts laughing and matches my pace. He increases the pace a little as I squeeze his hand and groan. Seeing

132

Logan up ahead, Kris waves and I stand up straighter. *No way. The manbear will NOT see me poop myself.* "Hey there Ms. Eldwin, how are things? Kristian, mind if I ask you something?" *Please stay here, both of you.* "Great, everything has been fantastic. 10 out of 10 stars. I should get going and let you two chat. I can make it on my own from here thanks." I continue walking as Kris tells him I'm not feeling well and something else I can't make out. *Cool story bro, but I got to GO.* I frown as I feel sweat form on my brow and pick up the pace to a brisk trot. *I feel like a Clydesdale.*

I clench my jaw as I continue down the path. *Please make it, please make it.* I exhale a sigh of relief as I see the B&B ahead. I think I hear someone say something, but I can't hear them over the sound of guts protesting that they can't hold it anymore. I cut through the path and wince as some briars catch on my legs. *Those are probably what they were yelling about.* I rush up to the stairs and hear a loud crack as my boot heel snaps. The porch light goes out as my ankle turns. I immediately slip and one of the porch decorations crumple under me as my knees hit the stairs. Thankfully, I feel no pain thanks to my 'clenched tight as steel' body. I grab the railing and pull myself up. *You can do this Sabrina.* Sweat drips from my nose and I grimace. I continue clenching as I crawl halfway up the stairs before I slip again. More sweat forms above my lip before finally making it up to the porch. *It doesn't matter how cute they are, I'm never wearing heels in the snow again, even if they are labeled as 'boots'.* I mentally chastise myself as I hobble to the door. *Please don't be locked.* I brace my hand against the frame as I turn the knob. *It's locked. I'm doomed. Wait, the kitchen!* I grimace and hobble along the porch to the back of the B&B. I hold onto the wall for support as I try to turn my butt cheeks into gates of something stronger than steel.

After opening the kitchen door, I rush inside only to slip on the tiled floor. I try to grab the wall for support, and slip on the snow from my boots. I slide down the wall and try to compose myself. *Okay Sabrina, you have made it this far, now drag yourself to that toilet!* The fireplace from the living room cast an eerie glow down the hallway. *I would be scared if I wasn't already dying inside.* I close the kitchen door with my foot and crawl over to the bathroom, my hands slipping on the melted snow. *Please. You are so close.* Raising up on my sore knees, I throw open the door and stand. Not even bothering to turn on the light as I barely make it to the toilet. *I don't want to see myself right now anyway.* I kick the door closed and close my eyes.

Once I feel confident there is nothing left to expel from my body, I wash my hands in the dark. *I'll look at myself after my shower.* I carefully walk out of the bathroom and make my way to the light switch. *I shouldn't leave melted snow for someone to slip on; I need a mop.* My head jerks as I hear yelling from outside. *Oh no, Luna!* I rush out through the kitchen door, momentarily forgetting about the broken heel of my boot. I stumble forward and catch myself on the porch railing. *Goodness Sabrina, how are you going to save anyone like this? Worse knightess ever.* I bite my lip and walk on my tip toes, wincing slightly. *Wait, I didn't actually hear Luna. What if someone was trying to break in?* I squint my eyes to look for something to use as a weapon. *I can barely see in front of me.* I blink a few times to hopefully help my eyes adjust to the dark.

The back porch light turns on as I dash towards the front. A man yells something from behind me as I am suddenly grabbed from the shadows. I push against the stranger and he grabs my throat, instantly stilling my movements. *I can't tell what he looks like.* I start to try and move him towards the light, but his gentle squeeze warns me to remain still. "I've got the intruder" An intense voice says loudly as he pulls me closer. His black hair shining in the moonlight as he looks down at me. *He thinks I'm an intruder!* I shake my head "I'm a guest" I say nervously, thankful he wasn't squeezing too hard. He instantly releases my neck, and I grip his arms to keep from falling. "My apologies, I tho-" He is cut off by Kris coming around the corner and swooping me into a hug. "Bri! Are you okay? What happened?" He says while looking me over, his face growing pale. I sway

134

and he holds my arms to steady me. "I don't even know what is happening right now" I say as the adrenaline starts to wear off after seeing him.

"We need to take her inside" The dark haired man says as Kris picks me up gently, cradling me as I bury my head in his coat. "Mr. Callahan, will you open the door for me?" I hear the door open as he carries me inside and sets me on the counter. Realizing who the man is now, I keep my eyes closed and groan as he asks where the first aid kit is. *Oh no, did I scratch the guest? Pecos even told me to keep my hands off the guests. To be fair though, he did choke me first. And with no dessert first.* I giggle as Kris looks me over. "Top drawer of the desk" Kris says with a clipped tone. "Let me unzip your coat. I need to make sure you aren't hurt anywhere else." I slowly opened my eyes to see him looking down at me with concern. *His eyes are so bright, they look silver.* He cups my cheeks and tells me to focus. I nod and reply, "It's mainly my ankle. I broke a heel and-" a scream cuts through the air and Kris quickly turns. I sway from the sudden movement and grab onto his arm. "I've got her" A deep voice says from behind him. Kris nods and rushes to the front door as Superman steps in front of my view.

I inhale sharply as I look over the planes of his face. I noticed first the chiseled angle of his jaw and cleft chin. His sharp nose poised above soft looking lips, with light green eyes that fade into dark blue. *My word, you're beautiful.* A lock of black hair curled against his forehead in rebellion from what appeared to be a well-maintained hair style. "We need to stop the bleeding; you look too pale." He says gently as I continue to look him over. *Whatever you say Superman.* "Okay. Wait, what bleeding?" I say, unable to focus. He frowns as Kris rushes in followed by Pecos holding a limp Luna in his arms. *Luna!* I move to slide down just as Mr. Callahan scoops me up and places me right back on the counter. I look up at him and then back down at my feet in shock *My feet never even touched the floor.* He shakes his head and tells me to wait. "She's fine, just passed out is all. Pecos take her to our room and get Willow" Kris says while moving things around. *I can't see thanks to Superman here.*

"I need you to take your coat off ma'am. You are bleeding and I need to see where it is coming from to stop it." Superman says with his voice stern now. "Oh. Okay." I say only partially registering his words. *Why does he sound like he is talking through water?* He moves to the side to help me with my coat as I gasp in horror at the kitchen. *There's blood everywhere.* Handprints were on the walls and floor with marks that looked as though someone had been drug through here. *What on earth happened?* I look down to see my black leggings soaked with snow and touch them gently. *That's not snow.* I think about the red covering my hand before everything fades to black.

CHAPTER TWENTY-SEVEN

~Logan~
Later

After loading up the ATV with the coolers, I drive back along the path to the outbuilding. *I'm glad I left the ATV by the clearing. Tonight seems to have gone well. Hopefully everyone had a good time and got some practice in.* I let my thoughts drift as I follow the path back to the outbuilding near the B&B. After unloading the ATV and locking it up, I glance at my watch and see that it's already after 11pm. *Time flies when you're having fun.* I walk towards the B&B, seeing the porch light turn on in the distance. *It must have blown earlier, Willow must have changed it already.* I walk through the clearing and freeze, seeing a vision from my worst nightmare. The porch lights illuminate blood all over the stairs and a broken lantern. *Did someone fall?* Rushing over I see blood on the floorboards covered what looks like multiple footprints. *Or was there a fight?* I narrow my eyes and look around. *I need to check inside.* As I walk towards the front door, I see blood on the knob and doorframe as though someone tried to get in. I look down and my stomach flips. *It looks like someone was drug to the kitchen.* Just as I lean around the corner, I see Mr. Callahan walking out of the kitchen with a bag. I curse as he jerks his head towards me.

Mr. Callahan looks at me and then down at the blood on his clothing. "Mr. Hale, I need you to stay calm for a moment." He says with a frown, as I start towards him. Kris walks out and I exhale in relief. "What happened?!" I all but roar as he grabs my

137

hand while leading me inside. "Calm down, Sabrina is asleep. Mr. Callahan had to stitch her up after she was cut by broken glass. We think she tripped going up the stairs and got cut on a lantern." I look at the blood spread throughout the kitchen as he drops my hand and hands me a towel. I grimace. *It's even on the cabinets.* "That's a lot of blood Kristian" I say with concern. "Mr. Callahan said she's okay for now, but she refuses to go to the hospital. She was fine with Mr. Callahan sewing her up here instead. He's a doctor." He adds hastily after seeing my look of confusion. *Did he have anything to give her for pain?* Kristian explains what happened as I frown and listen..

As we clean, Pecos comes out of our room to let us know he will be cleaning up outside. I groan remembering what outside looked like. "Willow never came down because Lunabella doesn't want her sister to know she fainted. They are both extremely queasy with blood so she didn't feel Willow would be able to help either. Lunabella will wait in your room until everything is cleaned up. She apologizes for them not being able to help with this" He adds the last part begrudgingly and I smile "Let her know it's not a problem at all and we respect her for knowing her limits." He nods and walks back into my room. After a few moments he goes outside. After we finish cleaning up the kitchen, Krist stretches, "We need to order more baking soda, maybe we should just keep a stockpile of it." Kristian says with a chuckle. "Someone should check on Sabrina." I say after washing my hands. He frowns and looks towards Mr. Callahan's cabin through the window. "I thought he would be back by now to check on her. He did mention he didn't want to be a doctor anymore. Maybe we should call someone local to do a house call?" He asks after a moment. I nod and Kristian pulls out his phone. "I'll make some calls." He goes through outside for better reception as I walk around to check for any stains I may have missed. *All clear.* I knock softly on my door, "Luna? It's Logan, everything is all cleaned up out here." I wait a moment before letting her know that I'm coming in.

I open the door slowly and poke my head in. *She's fast asleep on Pecos's bunk. Looks like it's boy's night in the living room.* I chuckle and close the door softly. I turn to get my coat "Might as well see if Pecos needs help cleaning up outside" I say while opening the front door.

CHAPTER TWENTY-EIGHT

~Thomas~
Earlier

The raven-haired woman looked down at her hand and swayed. I move back in front of her, cradling her head gently to my shoulder as she feints. "Where is the nearest clean bed?" I ask with impatience. *Better yet, where is the ambulance?* Mr. Graham points to a door, "That's her room-" I carefully scoop the woman up as I interrupt him "I need someone to get my black medical bag from the closet of my cabin." The man called Pecos nods and walks out the front door, careful of the snow/blood slurry on the floor. "You're a doctor? Is she going to be okay?" Mr. Graham asks while opening the door. I frown, "Yes I am, and I don't know. Mr. Graham, I need you to focus and do exactly as I say." I lay the women gently on the bed and proceed to explain all the things I will need. "Has anyone called for an ambulance yet?" I ask while placing her gently on the bed.

A pale hand touches my face, "No hospitals or ambulances. I accept this as my grave" the woman says seriously, her bright blue eyes staring into mine. Her hand falls down as her eyes close again. *Seriously? Who says that?* I narrow my eyes as Pecos walks in with my bag. He sets out the things I tell him to on the nightstand before going on another errand. *Glad I always keep a full bag on me, even if I am thinking about quitting the field.* The woman moans and opens her eyes. "Ma'am, can you hear me? I'm a doctor and I need to check your wounds. You are bleeding and I need to stop it" I say more clearly and she nods, "Sabrina,

140

my name is Sabrina. Can you fix me without a hospital or ambulance?" her bottom lip quivers and her eyes are filled with fear. "I have dissolvable stitches in my bag, but it will hurt a lot. Are you sure you don't want to go to a hospital?" I ask again as Mr. Graham walks back in with the items I requested. She nods, "I can do it" I sigh as I go to wash my hands. "Mr. Graham, would you mind waiting outside? It shouldn't take long. I'll need you to quickly change the bedding when I call for you" He looks at Sabrina and she gives him a thumbs up. He walks back to the kitchen, closing the door softly behind him.

After sitting down, I lean over and get the scissors from the metal tray. "I'm going to have to cut your dress and leggings to see where the bleeding is coming from" *She has already passed out again.* I curse as I quickly cut the clothing and see several cuts. "None look too deep, but I'll need to be sure there is no debris still in there" I put my gloves on and grab the forceps to pick the glass out, making sure to be thorough with tweezers afterwards. I quickly stitch the wounds; grateful she isn't conscious for this part. *I'm glad the fire isn't lit or I would be sweating.* After ensuring all wounds are closed, I clean her up and gently wrap her in clean sheet. I call out for Mr. Graham as I lift her carefully. He enters and immediately strips the bed. After he places a new fitted sheet, I set her down gently. "I need to make sure none of the stitches tore from moving her" I say as he nods and walks back out with a full garbage bag.

Once I finish checking my work, Sabrina's eyes open slowly. I smile and pull the blanket gently over her. "You did great Sabrina. Try not to move too much. I had to stitch up multiple lacerations." I reassure her. She smiles "Thank you. You look young for a doctor. Are you scouting for a potential honeymoon spot, perhaps?" I scoff at her boldness. *She's clearly in pain, but it's nice to be complimented I suppose.* "So, doctors must be elderly to be knowledgeable? All of that med school was for nothing it would seem. I'm thirty-five by the way." She frowns as I continue. "Also, are you saying that young doctors shouldn't seek out rest or relaxing vacations, unless it's for romance?

What about happily divorced young doctors? Are we allowed to rest?" I smirk as she registers my words. She apologizes and I see the sincerity in her eyes.

I exhale slowly and explain it was years ago, before I even knew what I wanted in life. I grab the water as she asks "So, what about now? They called you Mr. Callahan, meaning you weren't using your title when you booked your vacation. Do you not want to be a doctor anymore?" She holds the blanket to her chest and raises forward. I place my hand on her back to help her sit up. She straightens and almost hits my chin with her head. "Sorry, cold hands. You should move slowly for a while" I murmur while looking down at her. "That's not an answer" she replies, her eyes searching mine. I feel my lips twitch, "Usually a woman buys me dinner before asking these kinds of questions." She smiles and licks her lips before replying, "Usually men buy me dinner before choking me, but here we are." I laugh as she takes the water, sipping it slowly.

"Does that mean you want me to buy you dinner" I ask jokingly. "Is that a trick question? I'm clumsy, not blind. I also never turn down food." She replies seriously and I shake my head. "What happened to cause such a scene tonight?" I ask in hopes of changing the subject. *I can't start anything serious. No matter how gorgeous they are and especially not with a patient.* I repeat my thoughts in a mantra as she explains the events of the evening leading up to now. I regain my composure, as good doctors do, and reply "I see. You didn't even notice getting hurt, impressive. I'll be back to check on you later for signs of fever or infection" I stand and gather my things to sterilize back at my cabin. "Just use the door by the desk. It connects to the porch outside so it won't disturb everyone. I nod and walk out through the door she pointed at.

Pecos leans against the wall, watching me intently as I close the door softly behind me. "She needs rest, but she should be fine. I will be back later to check for signs of infection. She told me to use the private entrance later to avoid disturbing everyone. If anything seems wrong however, I'll wake the staff immediately." He nods before saying "Mr. Graham wants to see you". A blonde woman pokes her head out with her eyes closed. "Pecos?" she called. The tall man walks to her in long strides, "Sabrina is fine, but we haven't finished cleaning up the blood out here" he says while placing his arm under her hand. "I kept my eyes closed" I hear her reply before they head inside together. *What an interesting pair.* I shake my head and follow them inside.

Looks like he was in the middle of cleaning. "How is she? Also, is this safe to throw in the dumpster or do I need to take it somewhere to dispose of properly?" Mr. Graham asks as soon as I enter the kitchen. He holds up the bag of soiled bedding and I chuckle. "It's safe to throw away, so long as it doesn't attract local wildlife" He nods and I go over Sabrina's care, explaining she needs rest right now. "I'll be back later to check on her" *I need a shower.* I grab my medical bag and step outside. Turning, I see Mr. Hale clenching his fists. *Oh no, this looks really bad.* I look at the blood on my clothes and ask him to remain calm as he walks towards me.

Later

After my shower, I repack my bag with what I might need to fight an infection. I walk back to Sabrina's room, deciding to enter from the private entrance as she suggested. I knock on her door, but there's no answer. I press my ear to the door and hear groaning. *She could have fallen out of bed.* I let her know I am coming in as I open the door and shut it quickly to keep the chill out. I turn around, expecting to see Sabrina sprawled on the floor bleeding. What I wasn't expecting was to see her propped against the wall with her hair disheveled and her bra straps sliding off her shoulders. One hand braced behind her against the wall, the other under the blanket. *It's what I would be doing right now if I weren't here.* I feel my nostrils flare as her eyes lock onto mine and her lips part. Realizing that I was staring, I quickly turn around and apologize. My hand stills on the doorknob as I hear her say, "Don't go." I rest my forehead on the wall and close my eyes. *I need to go.* "Do you have any signs of infection?" I ask through gritted teeth, reminding myself it's perfectly normal to seek out pain relief. *Masturbation is a valid method, but not in front of the doctor.*

I hear movement behind me, and she hisses. I turn and rush to the bed "Where does it hurt?" I ask while setting my bag down. "Everywhere, so I've decided to fire you." I frown as she motions for me to lean down. I sit on the edge of bed and lean forward. She looks at me before saying low, "It would be improper of me to make advances on my doctor, so you're fired." I chuckle and shake my head. *So that's what she wants.* "What exactly are you looking for?" I ask and she relaxes slightly "Can you help with the pain, Superman?" I narrow my eyes, and she adds, "Don't worry, I've always preferred natural pain relief methods" Her ice blue eyes shine in the lamplight as she leans forward, her lips almost touching mine as she waits for my consent. *How chivalrous of you.* "I can't give you anything more than pain relief" I murmur, brushing my lips against hers. "Fine by me" she says. I fist my hand in her hair, tilting her head back as I devour her mouth. She moans as I deepen the kiss, gasping as I gently bite her lip. Her tongue flicks against mine and I groan against her mouth. Feeling my pants getting uncomfortably tight, I pull back and trail kisses along her jawline. After adjusting my position, I ask again what she wants from me as she arches her back. "Whatever you want to give me" she says as she drags my head back to her mouth. I smile against her mouth. *I can do that.*

I continue kissing her for a moment longer before pulling back, resting my forehead against hers as we catch our breath. I frown as I notice she has a thin sheen of sweat covering her. *She's fevered!* I curse and pull back as the door opens. Mr. Graham walks in followed by Mr. Hale, both wearing expresions of shock. "What's going on?" Mr. Hale asks sternly. "Why are you two just watching? Join us" Sabrina smiles at them as I cough. The two men look at each other in confusion. "Sabrina, are you alright? We called a local doctor and are waiting on a call back for a house call, but there is a long wait." Mr. Graham says while looking at me. I exhale as she argues she is fine. *They must be friends.* I contemplate looking up other lodges to stay in as they continue to banter.

Sabrina makes a noise and I look down at her, worried she strained herself. She turns her head up sharply, capturing my lips in a surprise kiss. "Sabrina!" Mr. Graham yells as Mr. Hale covers his twitching lips. I try to pull away, but my treacherous hand finds it way in her soft wavy tresses instead. "She seems fine now" Mr. Hale says with a chuckle. I pull back after realizing what happened. "See we all want the same thing. Stop over thinking things and come over here" she says while looking at the men by the door. She leans in again and I put my hands on her shoulders, "You're a beautiful woman, but you're hurt and possibly fevered. I need to check for signs of infection. Now is not the time" I say sternly as she pouts and lays back down.

I chuckle at her behavior. *She will probably be embarrassed later. I need to make sure her fever isn't too high, she could be hallucinating. It's also very hard to say no to her.* I reach into my bag and pull out the thermometer. She opens her mouth without me having to ask. *You are treating her, which makes her your patient.* I frown at the mental reminder before reading her temperature. "99.8 isn't a high fever, and it certainly wouldn't induce hallucinations" I murmur while frowning at her. Mr. Hale shakes his head and smiles at Sabrina. "She isn't hallucinating, she's just going after what she wants. Let us know if she needs anything. Besides an orgy" He grabs his friend's arm and tugs before whispering low, "We can talk to her later, come on." Mr. Graham sighs and closes the door behind them, leaving me alone with the sneaky temptress.

I narrow my eyes as said temptress relaxes against the wall. "Tell me you aren't interested and I'll stop." She says with a serious tone. *That's the problem, I don't know if I want you to stop.* I close my eyes, "Can you let me check your wounds before jumping me?" I reply with a defeated sigh. She grins, "Alright Doc, hurry up and get it over with so I can make out with Superman again" she says while crossing her arms under her bra clad breasts. *The black lace of her bra is in stark contrast to her skin.* I swallow and grab my bag from the foot of the bed before going to wash my hands. I make sure to splash my face and neck with cold water first. I walk out to see her laying down with the blanket tucked under her chin. Her head rests against the wall as she looks out of the window. I gently lifted the blanket off her leg, frowning as I notice small red dots on the sheet. I use a tongue depressor to gently apply ointment around her wounds, taking note of a few that were slightly inflamed. Once I finish checking all of her wounds, I re-cover her and quietly gather my things. *Glad she fell asleep before we went too far.* I sigh as I close the door behind me. "Mr. Callahan, how is she?" Mr. Graham stands and motions me to join them in the living room.

CHAPTER TWENTY-NINE

~Sabrina~

November 18th

6am

I wake up with the sudden urge to pee and stumble out of bed. *My legs are so weak.* I cry out in pain as my ankle rolls. I hit the floor and bite my lip. A door opens and I feel a pair of strong arms pick me up. "What do you need?" a familiar voice says, filled with concern. "Bathroom" I say while burying my head in Superman's shoulder. He carries me effortlessly to the bathroom. *How many times have you rescued me now?* "Can you stand?" he asks with concern. I look up at him and reply, "I think so." He sets me down slowly, making sure I can stand on my own before walking out. "I'll be right outside if you need anything." He closes the door, and I exhale as I quickly sit down to relieve myself.

I grimace at my reflection as I wash my hands. *I need a shower. At least he let me keep my undergarments on.* After brushing my teeth, I remove my underwear set. Using a damp rag, I wash my body, making sure to be careful of the stitches. *I can only clean some of me without it hurting.* I bite my lip remembering that I don't have any spare clothes in here. A knock on the door sounds before Superman says, "Don't overdo it, Sabrina." I put a hand on the door and counter to steady myself. "Don't come in. I'm taking it easy, but I saw dried blood. It had to go." He sighs and tells me he will get a sheet. I grip the counter as I feel myself start to sway. He knocks once and I open the door slightly. He shoves a sheet through the opening and tells me to call if I need help.

I smile and wrap it around me before leaning against the counter. "Superman?" I say weakly as my forehead breaks out in a sweat. The door opens and I feel myself being picked up carefully, my eyes suddenly feel heavier than ever. I feel my head lull onto his shoulder. "You've already stretched a few stitches and overexerted yourself. Let's not push it further" He walks over to the bed before setting me down gently. "I need to check to make sure you didn't tear anything" I mumble that I already checked while washing up and everything seemed fine. He frowns but agrees to trust me. "I'll wait to see if any red dots appear on the sheet. If they do, I'm going to need to check" he says sternly. I open my eyes and ask him how he knew I was in trouble. He looks towards the window and replies, "I was about to go for a jog. I've been checking on you periodically throughout the night." He says while smiling down at me. I frown and shake my head, only recalling the first time. "You were asleep for most of them, it was probably for the best" he adds softly. I yawn and he stands, "Try to stay in bed as much as possible today. I'll check on you again in a few hours." I try to nod but I'm so tired that I can't seem to move anymore.

8am

I wake up to someone knocking on the door "Sabrina? It's 8am. Would you like some breakfast?" Luna asks me before opening the door and poking her head inside. I shake my head, "No thanks, but can you bring me some clothes? Something easy to put on." I add as she walks inside, closing the door behind her. She nods as she walks to my dresser. She pulls out my silky dark purple bralette and panties set and grabs a long button up shirt from the bottom drawer. "That's perfect" I say while holding the blanket against my chest. She hands me the clothes before asking if I need anything else. "No thank you" I say. She closes the door behind her, and I throw the bralette over my head. I slip on the shirt next, buttoning it most of the way before even attempting to put on the underwear. *Come on knightess, you can do it, you can dress yourself!* I cheer myself on and smile.

I fling the blankets off me and slowly move my legs over the edge. "Alright Sabrina, you can do this." I lift my right leg slowly and try to lean forward. The stitches promptly say 'nope' and I whimper instead. I try to bend my leg, but that doesn't work for a different set of stitches. Furrowing my brows, I try with the other leg. *Ouch. Ouch. Ouch. OUCH!* I push through the pain and manage to get one leg through before hearing a ripping sound. I immediately clamp my mouth shut to keep from screaming as I feel my stitches rip open. I slide to the floor with tears flowing down my face. Pulling the sheet down to cover my lower half, I cry silently. *How silly I must look.* A whimper escapes as I close my eyes, unable to even curl up to cry. *You aren't a knightess or anyone's savior at all. You just keep making more trouble for others.* I lean my head back as the negative thoughts start to swarm me, not noticing the door opening or closing.

My eyes snap open as I feel fingertips wiping my cheeks, "Let's take care of this first" Superman says while tucking the sheet around my lower half. I shake my head, "You're supposed to be on vacation, not working from home. I should go to a hospital and stop bothering everyone." I say weakly. He frowns before helping me stand "Lean on me" he says firmly while putting my hands on his shoulders. I lean on him as he slowly squats down and grabs my underwear. *This is so embarrassing.* I raise each foot slowly as he slips my underwear over my ankles. He looks up at me with his gorgeous eyes and maintains eye contact. He carefully pulls my underwear upwards, keeping his hands under the sheet. *Amazing, he remembered where every stitch was and avoided them without even looking.* He stops mid-thigh before standing and lifting his gaze to the ceiling. I feel his hands on my waist, supporting me. "If you need more help, let me know" he says gently. I sniffle and thank him as I finish dressing.

I tell him I'm done and he looks down at me before tucking my hair behind my ear. "You don't have to go to the hospital. Just take it easy and let people help you" he says softly after setting me down on the edge of the bed. "Your wounds aren't very deep, but they are in areas where they can easily be reopened. You need to relax for the next few days if you want to avoid that. No more

149

trying to do everything yourself, especially if your goal is to make less work for people. Ask for help before you need serious help." He explains as he walks over to a locked box on my dresser. He opens it and puts some stuff on a tray before walking back towards me. "I left this in here last night *just in case* something like this happened." He set the tray on the nightstand and turned to wash his hands in the bathroom.

After getting everything ready, he applied a clear liquid on my reopened wounds. *It doesn't sting, that's good at least.* "I'm going to start now." He says as I look away to fight the tears. *I'm determined not to cry anymore.* My determination is apparently useless as I feel hot tears flowing down my face. He finishes quickly before asking me if I have any food allergies. I shake my head, "I can usually eat anything" I say and he nods. "You need to drink more water and eat more iron. You lost a lot of blood, that's why you're so weak right now. I'll go talk to the cook and see what's available" He walks out before I can tell him I'm not hungry. I look down and sigh. *When did he clean the floor?* I lean my head against the wall and close my eyes.

Later

A knock on the door wakes me and I blink a few times. I close my eyes again before hearing another knock. "Sabrina, I have breakfast. Mr. Jenkins brought-" I straighten and yell "Come in!" *I wonder what Mr. Jenkins brought.* Kris laughs and opens the door. "I told you the pastries would work" he says as he walks in with a green smoothie. "That's not a pastry" I complain as Logan walks in, shaking his head while holding a tray filled with food. I laugh as Kris sets the smoothie on the nightstand and Logan sets the tall tray over my lap. "What's all this?" I ask as I look at the food spread across the tray "Think of it as a bribe for you to hear us out. We need clarification on some things. I'll go first since I need to run to town in a bit." Kris says with an odd expression. I nod while slicing off some avocado.

Logan leans against the wall at the end of the bed as Kris sits next to me on the barstool. "Do you remember what happened last night? The part where you kissed Mr. Callahan and invited us all to an orgy, I mean" Kris asks me bluntly and I blush, nodding as I focus on placing my avocado slices on my toast. "Alright so you did in fact mean what you said about wanting all of us?" I nod again as Logan chuckles. Kris leans forward, "Like at once, or?" I cough at his question. The avocado plops back onto the plate and I sigh. Logan walks over and smacks Kris on the back of the head. "Seriously?" Logan asks him as I collect myself and my avacado. "I'm not saying I'm against it. I was just curious." He replies with a grin.

Logan moves to the foot of the bed, "What he should be asking is, could you clarify exactly what it is you want from each of us? Seeing you with Mr. Callahan made things a bit confusing after we just came to terms with you wanting both of us." Logan says as he moves to sit at the foot of the bed. I sigh and put my water down as the door opens. "I told you to drop the tray off, not interrogate her on her intentions" Superman says with a frown. "Actually, I can clear this up right now." They turn and look at me with various expressions. "I like all of you." I say while placing the avocado back on my toast. "I want to get to know each of you for whatever time we have together. I also want that time to be spent having fun. Interpret that whichever way you want, it's probably still accurate" I add while putting some cherry tomato slices on top of my avocado toast.

Another knock sounds and Luna pokes her head inside before saying, "Sabrina? I hate to interrupt, but your husband's office left a message for you. They said to tell you 'Daddy is coming and expects a decent mattress'. I went ahead and let them know that all of our mattresses are brand new." She pauses after seeing the tense expressions on everyone's face. "I'll let you go now." She closes the door as three pairs of eyes lock onto me. "You're married?!" they ask in unison. I groan and cover my face with my hands.

To be continued...

151

In loving memory of Reese. I wish depression hadn't taken
you before you were able to experience life as an adult.
I hope my stories can provide escapes for any who need them.

ABOUT THE AUTHOR

Kiki Holstad

Kiki Holstad is a young autistic woman from Georgia, currently overwhelmed with the state of the world. She just wants to have healthy food, live debt free, and write in the mountains with her fat cat and hyper golden retriever. Her goal is to provide stories that entertain people. She does not do any special marketing or advertisements. If you like her books, please buy one for your local library and spread the word.
She has no sponsorships or endorsements (anything mentioned in the book was not paid to be mentioned). She does not use AI nor have an editor, so if you find any errors with her books, please let her know via email and she will fix it ASAP.

You can email her to sign up for book releases/newsletters at kikiholstadbooks@gmail.com.

Please note: Kiki is not active on social media and will only use it to post updates related to her books. If you see any suspicious activity, please reach out to her directly via email.